THE DEMON OF SALFRAN BAY

Naomi Stebbins

ISBN: 979-8-89694-198-9 - paperback

ISBN: 979-8-89694-199-6 - ebook

It was a long, quiet drive to Salfran Bay.

Mark stared out the window at the endless forest surrounding the ashen, concrete roads. As the sun faded into the trees, he watched the sky darken from a soft pink into a rich, dark blue dotted with stars.

The car was silent, save for Rick's occasional snort and sniffle.

"We'll be there in 10." He finally grunted.

Mark gave a brief hum in response.

Eventually, they pulled into a narrow driveway, and after Rick fumbled a bit with his car keys, they parked in his garage. Mark climbed out of the car at Rick's request and followed Rick into his small, blue house.

"Your room's down the hall," Rick gestured to his right. "Get changed, unpack your stuff, and go to bed. I'll take you to school at seven."

Mark nodded. He briefly debated saying goodnight, but Rick had already turned away, trudging up the stairs.

He dipped into what was now his room, flipping the light off, stripping down to his boxers, and slipping into bed. He lay alone in the dark, staring up at the ceiling, exhausted out of his mind, but unable to close his eyes. By the time the hum of the AC finally put him to sleep, it was beginning to get lighter.

When he woke up the next day, his dreams slipped away from his memory, but the terror and misery still lingered for a while.

At eight, Mark found himself seated in the waiting room of the Salfran Bay High main office.

"Marcus Langley?" A plump, middle-aged woman with blonde hair and rosy cheeks stuck her head out the door.

Mark nodded, and at the woman's request, followed her down a short corridor into an office. The lady sat behind her desk, and Mark sat across from her.

"So," The woman's cheeks puffed when she smiled. "Welcome to Salfran Bay! I'm your guidance counselor, Ms. Muff! I'll be making sure you get all settled in here at school."

"Mhm."

"Now, I know it's a bit difficult, transferring in the middle of the year, so I arranged for–"

Mark heard a knock at the door.

"Oh! Speak of the devil!" Ms. Muff stood, shuffling to the door.

She opened the door, and a short, skinny boy with comically big glasses and curly brown hair walked in.

"Lincoln, pull a chair up?" The boy nodded, picked up a chair from the front of the office, and brought it to the desk.

"Now, why don't you two introduce yourself to each other?"

"I'm Mark," Mark said, picking at a patch of dead skin on his hand.

"I am Lincoln," the boy replied, still not looking at Mark. He spoke in a monotone, his voice somehow simultaneously gravelly and squeaky.

"...maybe a fun fact?" Ms. Muff asked hopefully.

Lincoln narrowed his eyes. "Ducks have corkscrew penises."

Mark choked on his spit.

Ms. Muff, looking more defeated than taken aback, spoke again. "...about yourself, sweetie."

"I find it interesting that ducks have corkscrew penises."

Mark silently scooted his chair away from Lincoln.

"...how about you, Mark?"

"I... I like drawing?"

"Right, that's nice...anyway, Lincoln's in your grade, so I thought it'd be nice if he showed you around the school!"

Mark stared at Ms. Muff in disbelief. *Why the hell would you think that?*

"The cafeteria is there. The library is there. The music room is there." Lincoln led Mark around the first floor, nodding at various rooms as they passed by.

"The ninth-grade classes are on the next floor, the tenth-grade classes are on the next next floor, the eleventh-grade classes are on the next next next floor, and the twelfth-"

"Yeah, I got it. I'm... I'm gonna go now." Mark quickly took the opportunity to get away from the boy who almost certainly had an indecent attraction to avians.

He walked up the stairs, found his way onto the eleventh-grade floor, and turned into a classroom with the telltale number 403 marked above its door.

He walked into a scene he'd seen a thousand times at a hundred different schools. Kids were seated at desks around the room, some gabbing obnoxiously, some sitting in silence. An older woman was standing at the front of the room, silently observing the class.

Mark walked up to her. "Hey. I'm new."

"Oh. Right. Marcus?"

"Mark's fine."

"I'm Ms. Dover. You can sit over there." She pointed at a small desk in the back corner of the room.

Mark nodded and sat down. He stared out the window as the teacher began droning about something Mark couldn't be bothered to listen to.

"Hey. You got a pencil?" A voice whispered next to him.

Mark turned to face a girl with light green hair seated just to his right. She wore a black crop top and matching denim shorts and had a silver piercing on the shell of her right ear.

"Yeah." Mark rifled through his bag and pulled out the one pencil he had that wasn't completely chewed up.

"Thanks, man." She gave him a toothy grin as she took the pencil from him. "So you're new here, right?"

"...Yeah."

"Nice. I'm Ellie, by the way. How about you? Where're you from?"

Mark pursed his lips. "Calculus, remember?" He nodded at the teacher.

"...This is English." Ellie rolled her eyes, still smiling. "Whatever. I can take a hint."

Mark stared at the girl for a moment, before he went back to looking out the window, idly wondering how he had gotten the two subjects mixed up. The Charles Dickens prominently featured on the whiteboard was the creator of the Pythagorean Theorem, was he not?

His next few classes were as dull as he expected. He tuned out every teacher who spoke for an extended amount of time in favor of spacing out or mindlessly scribbling in his notebook.

At around two o'clock, Mark had slipped out of class to ostensibly go to the bathroom, though in reality, he wandered around the halls without any real aim.

Just as he was about to turn a corner, the sound of something solid hitting metal rang through the air.

Mark quickly ran up to see a tall, muscular boy standing by a locker, clutching a much smaller kid by his head.

Mark stiffened, recognizing who the smaller boy was.

Small school.

Sneering, the taller boy hit Lincoln's head against the locker with another loud bang. Even with his head turned Mark could make out the blood dripping down Lincoln's head.

When it fully registered in his head just what he was looking at, without thinking, Mark sprinted toward the scene.

"Hey!" Mark shouted. "*What the hell are you doing?*"

The tall kid turned to Mark, momentarily looking taken aback before he smirked at him.

"This bastard," the boy nodded at Lincoln, who at that point, he had let go, "owes me twenty bucks. But he wouldn't pay up."

"I'm not going to." Lincoln suddenly spoke up. Despite the nasty gash on his head, he only looked mildly disconcerted at best. "I'm not going to give you money." The tall boy's hand darted out toward Lincoln.

"Don't." Mark yelled.

The boy turned to look at Mark, a snarl beginning to form on his face. Mark was suddenly extremely aware of the fact that the kid was twice his size.

"You can't tell me what to do, jackass." The kid advanced toward him. "Do you have a death wish?" A twisted grin formed on his face, and Mark's throat went dry.

He prepared himself for a fight, awkwardly putting his fists up, but before anything could transpire, the sound of the bell rang through the hallway.

The boy pulled back, annoyed, as hundreds of kids began pouring out of class.

"You got fucking lucky." The kid stormed away, his feet thumping against the floor.

Mark, a bit stunned, stared after him for a moment, before he turned to Lincoln, blood still running down his forehead, who had an unreadable expression on his face.

They looked at each other for a long moment in silence, before Lincoln finally spoke.

"Thank you." Without another word, he briskly walked away from Mark.

"So, how'd your day go?" Rick asked absently, drumming his fingers against the steering wheel.

"...Fine."

After a few moments of silence, Mark heard a few drops of rain tap against the windshield, before hundreds more poured down in rapid succession, the wipers beginning to squeak against the window in response.

"Fucking... forecast was bullshit." Rick angrily tapped the car radio, muting the weather channel. Several minutes of silence ensued before they pulled into Rick's garage. Mark followed Rick inside the house, finding his way into his room.

Seating himself on the foot of his bed, Mark cracked his suitcase open, rifling through his belongings, before he pulled out a pencil and his sketchbook. It was very much worn, with the edges of its cover bent and curled, and several pages sticking out of the book. Mark turned to the first clean page, and looking out the window, tried to replicate the backyard outside on the paper.

It was a small, ordinary scene. A tall picket fence surrounded a shaggy, untrimmed patch of grass, now dampened by the rain, which had gone as soon as it had come. There was a barbecue tucked in the corner of the yard, and a skinny, barren tree stood in the middle of it all.

Mark spent a few hours sketching the yard, trying to recreate every bit of detail, no matter how small or insignificant.

When he finally finished, he held the sketchbook up next to the window so that the backyard and his replica appeared to be the same size.

He couldn't help but smile when he realized how similar they looked.

As Mark walked through the woods, he savored the noises he heard.

The owls hooting, the crickets chirping, and the trees rustling echoed through the crisp night air, all contributing to the familiar ambiance that Mark relished.

Whenever Mark was moved to a new place, he always tried to go to the nearest forest at least once. He had always found an oasis in the verdancy that would surround him, in the creatures that would scamper or fly through the woods.

And yet, every forest Mark had been to was different. He remembered the scorching heat that blazed through the Griss Woods in Florida and the painful chill of the Minnesotan North Park. He remembered getting lost for hours in the vast Abraham Forest of South Carolina, and how almost as soon as he had entered the Colorado Worth Pines, he had left.

But despite it being ever-changing depending on the time and place, nature was one of the few pleasurable constants in Mark's life, and Mark would always love and appreciate it.

A smile was forming on his face when the peace of the night was shattered by a scream of unmistakable agony.

Mark stiffened for a painful moment before instinctively sprinting toward the source of the sound as fast as he could.

"Hey, *hey!* Who–" As Mark jerked to his left, he stopped in his tracks, staring at the sight before him.

A man, who couldn't have been much older than Mark, was sprawled out on the ground before him, his limbs twisted against the ground, his eyes glazed over with a lifeless fog. Blood pooled around his upper body, bubbling at the gash at his neck where it was pouring out of.

Mark doubled over, letting out a sound part way between a scream and a gag. He was holding back vomit before he heard the crack of a branch ring through the air.

Mark snapped up to face a masked, bloodied figure clutching a pocket knife, standing not even ten feet away.

"Help! HELP! HELP!"

After what seemed an eternity of running, he made it out of the woods and back to town, a small crowd of people staring at him as he emerged.

"Hey, kid!" A short man with graying hair ran up to him. "What–"

Mark doubled over, breathing heavily. "There– there's a guy! And, he's dead, and there was someone–" His breaths became shorter, and Mark couldn't get another word out.

"Okay, breathe, *breathe*." The man put his hand on his shoulder, and Mark flinched away.

Eventually, his breathing slowed, and he stood upright.

"Okay. *Okay.* I... I was walking through the woods, and I heard a scream. I ran over... and there was this guy... he was bleeding, I think he was dead, and... there was someone... they were holding a knife, and... and I think they killed him."

The crowd that had gathered around began to yell. Someone shouted to call the police.

The next few hours were a blur. People asked him questions, which he numbly answered. An ambulance and a police car came to the scene, and he was taken away.

Now, Mark found himself seated in a small, gray room, with only a table and the chair he was seated in inside it. Mark rubbed his biceps, trying to ease the chill.

After a few minutes, he heard a knock at the door, before a tall, lanky cop walked in.

"Okay... Marcus." He said, glancing at a paper he held. "We're going to have to ask some questions about what you saw, and then, we'll try to send you on your way. Is that alright?"

Mark nodded, and proceeded to recount everything that had happened to him in the last couple of hours.

"...And why were you out that late?"

"I... I was bored. And Rick said it was fine."

"Rick?"

"Um, my foster dad."

"Right."

The cop rifled through some papers before they heard the door knock. A mousy woman stuck her head through the doorway.

"Wade, you gotta check this out."

The officer, apparently named Wade, stared at the woman in disbelief. "Cara, I'm in the middle of-"

"I wouldn't be calling you if it wasn't important." Wade scoffed but stood anyway. "I'll be back in a few minutes," he said, nodding at Mark as he left the room.

Mark rested his entire upper body on the table, pressing the side of his face against its surface.

Contrary to what Wade had said, Mark spent nearly an hour in confinement before he returned.

"So," Wade pursed his lips as Mark sat up. "Are you sure about what you saw?"

"Yes," Mark replied, exasperated.

Wade pinched the bridge of his nose. "Look, I'll get to the point. It was suicide."

Mark felt his mouth fall open a bit, and he stared at Wade dumbly for a long moment.

"What?" He finally asked. "No. No, it wasn't. I- I *saw* someone-"

"He cut his own neck. The autopsy confirmed it."

"But that- I *saw* him. He was covered in blood, and he was holding some kind of *knife*-"

"Look. I get it. You saw something messed up, and you were freaking out. Obviously, it'd be normal if you were seeing things."

"Seeing things- no! I wasn't *fucking* seeing things! I saw... I..." Mark trailed off.

It was dark. He was still reeling from the sight of the mangled body. He had only looked at the figure for a split second before running off.

No... I know what I saw. It-

"You know, we looked you up. We know about your records."

"Records?"

Wade pulled out yet another file, cracking it open. "C-PTSD, BPD, depression, psychosis..."

Mark's blood chilled. "What- *how'd you get that?*"

"The state keeps them filed." Wade looked at Mark with a pity that made him want to throw up. "Okay, what you saw- it wasn't your fault. And it's not your fault that you're..." he waved his hand over the file. "But, Marcus, what you saw... it wasn't real. You gotta know that."

"No, you-" Mark bit his tongue.

He wanted to tell Wade that the only reason those diseases were on file was because he lived his whole life with sick fucks that didn't want to deal with him. He wanted to scream that he wasn't insane. That everything he had witnessed coincided with reality.

But people like Wade never listened to him.

"Your foster dad's here. We'll let you go back home, okay?" Wade looked at Mark with a small smile on his face.

Mark could only numbly nod.

Rick didn't say a word the entire ride back. The silence was both a blessing and a curse.

"Get some rest, Mark." He finally said when they got back. Without another word, Mark and Rick both retired to bed.

He didn't sleep a wink that night.

The next morning, the moment he stepped into school, hushed whispers broke out all around him.

Mark knew exactly why he was suddenly the subject of everyone's interest. He stared down at the floor and speed-walked through the halls, trying to be as inconspicuous as possible.

Homeroom was no better. When he opened the door, nearly everyone in the classroom stopped to gawk at him for a good few moments. Mark quickly slid into his seat.

Most of the conversations that swarmed through the room drowned each other out, but the few bits and pieces he could hear, unsurprisingly, centered around him, murder or both.

However, he was very aware of a girl, seated only one or two desks away from him, gabbing loudly to the boy next to her. "That guy, Mark? You heard what he did, right? God, what a psycho." At that, the girl turned to Mark and sneered at him, and he glared at her in turn.

She turned back to her friend. "I bet he was just looking for attention. Either that, or he's crazy. You-"

"Hey." A voice cut her off, and Mark turned to see Ellie standing in front of the girl, glaring down at her.

"He's sitting *right there*, you jackass." Ellie nodded at Mark, before turning back to the girl.

The girl sputtered a bit, before saying something inaudible to Ellie. Ellie walked away, and the sulking girl stopped talking to her friend. She slid into the seat next to Mark, smirking.

"Perks of being popular. You can get anyone to shut up."

"I didn't need that." He finally bit out, snarling a little to get the point across.

Ellie frowned, looking taken aback. "Oh. Uh... sorry, I didn't—"

"Didn't you say you could take a hint?" Mark cut her off, looking away from her.

Ellie was quiet for a bit. "You're right— I can." She didn't speak again after that.

Mark briefly glanced at Ellie, staring down at her desk. He tried to ignore the inkling of guilt stirring in his stomach.

Mark sat at an otherwise unoccupied table tucked in the corner of the cafeteria, picking at his food.

He had evaded the persistent attention on him relatively well, though it was still undeniably present. However, during lunch, his schoolmates seemed more inclined to let him be. Mark idly listened to the mindless chit-chat floating through the air, trying to drown out his own thoughts.

"Hello."

He turned his head around to face Lincoln, standing directly behind him, a large bandage now plastered on his forehead.

Mark glared. "What do you want?"

Lincoln took an uninvited seat next to him before replying. "You weren't lying. Were you?" When Mark didn't respond, Lincoln elaborated. "About the man you saw. That killed Eric–"

"Eric?" Mark asked stupidly.

"His name. Eric Jacobs." Lincoln folded his hands together in his lap, staring down at them. "And you weren't lying."

"...Okay, who put you up to this?"

"Nobody." Lincoln replied, still looking down at his hands. Mark opened his mouth, forming a retort in his head, before taking a good look at Lincoln.

Despite his lack of expression, there was something genuine in his face. Mark couldn't put his finger on what it meant, but it was there.

"...You better not be screwing with me." Mark said, lowering his voice a level.

"The cops said I was crazy. But I swear to *God*, there was someone standing there–"

"And are you sure they killed him?"

Mark scoffed. "He was holding a knife and he was covered in blood. Yeah, I'm sure." Mark sighed shakily. "...Do you believe me?" He asked, softly.

Lincoln nodded.

"I...that's..." Mark looked away, not knowing how to finish his sentence.

Lincoln hummed but was otherwise silent for a bit. "Okay. I'll help you."

Mark tilted his head. "Help me... what?"

"I'll help you find out who killed Eric."

"...what?" Mark stared at Lincoln in disbelief. "Someone killed Eric. The police won't solve the murder. But someone has to. And we're the only ones that can, since we know he was–"

"Wait, *wait*." Mark glared at Lincoln, who still wasn't looking at him. "The hell are you talking about?"

"Like I said, the police won't solve the murder. But somebody has to. And we're the only ones that know he was murdered." For once, Lincoln turned to meet Mark's eyes. "So we have to be the ones to do it."

"I—" Mark sputtered. "You can't be fucking serious. This isn't a movie, you…"

"I know that, because of the lack of cameras."

"The hell is wrong with you?"

"That is confidential information."

At that, Mark stood with enough force that he banged his side against the table, and he was sure he had bruised it. Grabbing his lunch tray, he began to storm off.

"The bell hasn't rung yet." Lincoln said.

As if on cue, the bell rang.

Lincoln glanced up at the ceiling. "…Okay."

After he was dismissed by the police, Mark had no idea what he was going to do next.

Now, in the present, as he completely tuned everything in class out, he was forced to fully confront that reality.

Was he just going to go on, as if he hadn't witnessed a murder, keeping what he had seen to himself? Mark was fully aware of how awful that'd be, but he couldn't think of anything else for the life of him.

Half the town thought he was insane. He couldn't call emergency services. The only person in Salfran Bay who believed what he said was clearly mentally ill.

Mark screwed his eyes shut. Lincoln was insane. There was no questioning it. They were two dumb kids in a town Mark couldn't even find on Google Maps. They couldn't solve a murder. Mark knew this.

But the image of the mangled corpse kept searing its way through his mind.

Every memory Mark had of the body came back a bit differently. How windy it was, how the leaves crackled under his feet, how much or little he could see, all the fine details were repeatedly distorted with time and newfound thoughts and feelings. He'd never be able to truly relive the sight of the murder.

The only true constant was the corpse itself, but even that started to change. Every time Mark's mind wandered back to the forest, its lifeless eyes became a little more pleading. Its mouth pried open a little more, and its silent cry became a little louder.

And in the present, when Mark thought back to it, it seemed to be screaming for help. For justice.

The moment the bell rang, Mark slipped out of the classroom, looking around the hall for the boy with the telltale curly hair. Sure enough, he was walking at the end of the hall, just about to turn a corner. Mark ran up to him, grasping his shoulder.

"I need to talk to you." Mark said.

Lincoln nodded.

The two then went out to the back lot. Mark rested his back against the wall of the school, while Lincoln stood off a few feet away from him.

"Okay, I have no idea how this is gonna work." Mark started. Lincoln hummed in response.

"And if we're being honest, we're probably going to fuck this up. But someone's dead. I... I can't just do *nothing*."

"You want to work with me." Lincoln said bluntly.

"...Yeah. I guess." Mark rolled a strand of his hair between his fingers.

"Good."

The air was silent for a long moment.

"So... where exactly do we start?"

"I have two ideas. You won't be opposed to the first one, but I think you'll hate the second one." Mark frowned. "...What's the second one?"

"You'll hate it."

Mark glared. "What is it?"

"You'll hate it."

"...I swear to god–"

"We break into the town morgue, and perform our own autopsy on the corpse."

"...what."

"You hate it." Lincoln nodded.

"How would that even– why?"

"We can confirm it wasn't a suicide, determine the cause of death, and subsequently narrow our list of suspects."

"I... that's..."

The idea was blatantly insane. Not even a few hours ago, Mark would have vehemently opposed the idea, and gotten away from Lincoln as quickly as possible.

But it also occurred to Mark that, a few hours ago, he wasn't trying to solve a murder.

"Fuck it. I'll do it." Mark said, defeated.

For the first time since Mark met him, Lincoln looked genuinely surprised, though he quickly regained his composure.

"...Okay, then. Are you free Saturday?"

Mark had just cracked the front door open when Rick called out to him.

"Where are you going?" He turned around to face Rick, crossing his arms.

"I... just out. Walking."

"Where?" Rick persisted.

Mark thought for a moment before replying. "Long Avenue." It wasn't exactly a lie.

Rick pursed his lips before nodding. "Okay... be careful. And be back by 7:00." Mark nodded and walked out of the house.

There wasn't a sliver of blue in the cloudy sky. As Mark walked along Long Avenue, he could hear the wind whistling through the air.

Using his phone and the address Lincoln had given him, he eventually found his way to a small, gray building at the edge of town, with a simple sign reading 'SALFRAN BAY MORGUE' hanging above its front entrance.

"There you are." Lincoln's voice rang through the air as he walked towards him.

"Can't believe I agreed to this..." Mark grumbled to himself, before turning to Lincoln. "Okay, so how is this going to work?" Lincoln looked down.

"We find a way into the morgue. Then, we look for the body. Then, we conduct an autopsy–"

"Okay, wait." Mark scoffed. "What the hell do *you* know about autopsies?"

"I took several online courses centered around biomedical science." Lincoln replied. "While I doubt I will be able to determine the details of Eric's death as well as a medical professional, I'm confident that I'll at least be able to get some idea of what happened."

"I- fine." Mark slumped his shoulders in defeat.

The two walked up to the entrance. Lincoln tried to open the glass doors to no avail.

"It's locked. We–"

"Hang on, I think I got it." Mark pulled out two bobby pins. He twisted them into shape, before carefully sliding them into the lock. After a few moments, the door clicked open.

Lincoln stared at Mark. "...Steady hands," Lincoln murmured. "Steady, *steady* hands..."

Mark tilted his head at Lincoln, before opening the door.

After walking down a hallway so short it might as well not have been there, Mark and Lincoln stood in front of a white door with a rusted push bar, a small window near the top of it, fogged over to the point where it revealed nothing.

Pushing the rusted bar, they walked into the room, where Mark was immediately hit by a gust of cold, but it quickly faded into a mild chill.

As the door closed behind them with a click and a thud, he looked around the morgue.

In the center of the room, there was a large metal table, with rust at its corners. To the right of it, there were a series of sinks against a wall, and a cart full of medical supplies– most of which Mark doubted he could name. To the left of it, there was a wall with a series of square doors lined up in two rows across it, and Mark, with a shiver, realized exactly what was behind them.

"How..." Mark walked up to the series of doors, Lincoln at his side. "How do we know which one is Eric's?"

"Look closely." Lincoln replied.

Mark squinted and realized that on every door, there were small labels with names on them.

"Eric Jacobs." Mark said, staring at one of the labels. "That him?"

"Yes."

Taking a deep breath, Mark cracked the door open to face a pair of bare feet, the rest of the corpse's legs obscured by a white cloth. The body seemed to be laid out on what appeared to be a long, metal tray.

"Can you help me...?" Mark pulled at the tray, glancing at Lincoln.

Lincoln rose an eyebrow. "Lift the body?"

"Yes."

Lincoln nodded. "Yes, I can." Lincoln grabbed a hold of the side of the tray as Mark pulled it out.

With a collective grunt, they lifted the tray, before, at Lincoln's instruction, placing it on the metal table.

"Okay," Mark said, panting a little. "Now what?"

"I'm going to conduct the autopsy." Lincoln walked over to the cart, pulling it next to the table. He put on a pair of latex gloves as he spoke. "If you want to look away, I understand."

"I–" Mark stared at the cloth, feeling his throat going dry. For the first time, it fully registered that underneath the cloth was the same mutilated body that had sent him into a terror he hadn't felt for years.

"Again, if you want to look away, I–"

"I heard you," Mark bit out. "I'll loo– I'll *help*."

Lincoln looked at Mark, making eye contact. "Are you sure?"

"Yes." Mark replied, a bit exasperated.

Lincoln looked away. "Okay." He pulled the cloth down to the corpse's waist.

The corpse had been cleaned up since Mark saw it. One would be forgiven for thinking that Eric was simply in a deep sleep, had it not been for the way that his skin was blanched with death, or the gash at his neck– but even the wound was cleaned, and it now amounted to a thick, crimson line across his throat.

And yet, it was unmistakably the same maimed corpse Mark had seen that night.

Lincoln stared at the wound. He gently ran a finger over the laceration.

"It wasn't a suicide." He finally said. "It's impossible with the angle."

Mark tensed at the confirmation. The rush of relief at the validation of what he saw was immediately drowned out by his own confusion.

"But... why'd they say it wasn't?"

"The coroner was either very incompetent... or they were lying."

"Lying... did someone pay them off, or something?"

"It's possible." Lincoln said. "Again, they could have just been very bad at their job."

Mark didn't answer and watched Lincoln continue his work. After performing a series of odd procedures with the medical equipment, he spoke up again.

"Eric died at approximately 9:30 that night. That was around when you found him, right?"

Mark rolled his eyes. "We already know all this. It doesn't–"

"Please answer the question."

"Yeah. I did. So what? We already knew this. It doesn't get us anywhere."

"If you happen to have more knowledge regarding biomedical science than I do, feel free to take over."

Lincoln worked for a few more minutes before placing the tools he held back into the cart.

"I can't figure anything else out. We have to go on that alone."

Mark stared at Lincoln in disbelief.

"...*that's it?*" he snarled. "You– you made me break into a fucking *morgue*. Do you know how much *shit* that could get me into? I'm already on thin ice with the state! And that's *all* you can tell me? The HELL is wrong with you?" Mark was about to shout again, but he stopped himself when he saw the way Lincoln was staring at the ground.

"...I'm sorry." Lincoln said, in a low voice.

The pitiable look on his face quickly made Mark's anger fizzle out.

"I... it's–"

"I couldn't do this, but I took you here anyway. And I'm sorry."

"I–" Mark cut off, feeling that familiar, uncomfortable guilt that he hated.

"You tried." Lincoln was still looking at the floor.

Mark, awkwardly, moved to touch Lincoln's shoulder.

"I mean, you did better than I would've. That's–"

"Let's put it back." Lincoln nodded at the corpse, pulling away from Mark.

"R-right." Mark and Lincoln lifted the metal tray, pushing it back into the fridge they'd pulled it out of.

After they shut the door, Mark opened his mouth to say something but stopped when he heard the muffled but unmistakable sound of chatter, coming from outside the room. Mark stared at Lincoln, panicked.

With superhuman speed, Lincoln pushed the cart into the corner of the room, so that there was a small space between it and the wall. Mark and Lincoln quickly ducked behind the cart.

"*You said this place was closed,*" Mark hissed.

Lincoln opened his mouth to reply, but he was cut off by the sound of the door opening.

Peeking through a space between the medical supplies, he watched a woman with graying hair walk into the room, and a younger, anxious-looking man trailing behind her.

"Is this the only way to do this?" The man asked, wringing his hands together. "Couldn't we *just* get rid of the body?"

The woman placed a large, red can on the center table. "People will ask questions. A corpse going missing?" The woman snorted. "Someone will put two and two together."

"But wouldn't Eric–"

Mark stiffened at that, glancing at Lincoln, who simply nodded at him in response.

"No one's gonna bat an eye at a fire. They happen here all the time." The woman turned the can over, pouring the contents all over the ground, thankfully avoiding the corners of the room in favor of its center.

Mark immediately recognized the pungent stench. *Gasoline.*

"Come on, Arnie." The man and woman hurried out of the room, leaving Mark and Lincoln behind the cart.

But before they shut the door, the woman threw a lit match into the center of the room, and the next thing Mark knew, the room surrounding them was lapped up by flames.

Mark screamed, simultaneously shooting up and backing into the corner. He accidentally kicked the cart forward, and it was immediately engulfed by the fire.

"WHAT THE HELL?!" Mark shrieked.

"Window!" Lincoln yelled, gesturing to his left. There, there was a window just off to the side, its surrounding areas untouched by the fire.

Mark sprinted over to the window, frantically scrambling to push it open, but to no avail.

"It's locked!" Mark shouted.

"Break it!"

Mark tore his jacket off and wrapped his fist in it, before hitting the window as hard as he could. After a few tries, it was completely destroyed.

"COME ON!" Mark climbed into the window frame, leaping out of the building, Lincoln following suit.

The two sprinted inhumanly fast, not even stopping when they were a safe distance from the building. The next thing Mark knew, the two of them were standing in a neighborhood almost half a mile away from the scene.

Mark doubled over, before moving to crouch on the sidewalk. "What the hell *was* that!?"

Lincoln looked down at him. "Mark, calm down–"

"I almost– I COULD'VE DIED!" Mark could hear his heart pounding in his ears, his breaths growing quicker to the point of hyperventilation. He put his hands over his mouth, instinctively trying to slow his breathing, but the attempt was drowned out by his own panic.

"Mark, Mark," Lincoln crouched down but still kept a distance from Mark. "We got away from the fire. The fire is gone. You will be okay. Please breathe."

Mark curled in on himself tighter, but eventually, his breathing slowed a bit.

"Mark, I am going to ask you a question, and I want you to answer it. How does a strawberry taste?"

Mark scoffed, still quivering.

"W-what are you even–"

"Please."

"I... it's... it depends, I guess. Sometimes they're a little sour, but the good ones taste... sweet. Juicy. But even the good ones are a little... tangy. I mean, not tangy, but..."

Mark's breaths were now stable. "...yeah."

"Okay. Stand please."

Slowly, still shaking a bit, Mark stood.

"Sorry." Mark shook his head. "I don't know what that was–"

"You were having a panic attack." Lincoln replied.

Mark stared at Lincoln, before scoffing. "What? No. That... that just happens sometimes. It... it wasn't..."

"It's common for people to have at least one throughout their life. There's nothing wrong–"

"It wasn't a–!" Mark bit the words out, before cutting himself off. "It... it doesn't matter. Are we *not* gonna talk about what happened back there?"

Lincoln looked down at the sidewalk, wringing his hands together.

"The man and the woman burnt the morgue down. It had something to do with Eric's death." Lincoln paused for a bit, before continuing. "The man said something about getting rid of a body. It can be inferred they meant Eric's body..."

"They were... they burnt it down to get rid of it? But why..." Mark trailed off, as realization crept up on him.

"They didn't want anyone to find out about the cause of death." Lincoln said quietly, voicing Mark's thoughts.

"Did– did someone pay them off?" Mark asked. "The killer?"

"Maybe." Lincoln hummed. "Or... one of them is the killer. Or a close affiliate of theirs."

"I–" Mark cut off. "Shit, you're right."

"Either way, it's safe to assume that they have some involvement in the murder."

"So... what do we do now?" Mark asked. "We can't call the cops– we'd have to tell them *why* we were there, and that'd– we can't."

"I'm aware." Lincoln looked up at Mark. "We have to confront them directly."

"What– but they–they burnt down a *fucking* morgue." Mark sputtered. "We can't just–"

"Mark, I'm aware of the risks, but we don't have a choice." Lincoln looked directly into Mark's eyes. "If you don't want to come, I understand. I–"

"You–" Mark pursed his lips. "I can't just... I'm stronger than you." Mark said, dumbly. "And... I can't let you do shit like that alone– I–" Mark rubbed his temple. "Do you– do you at least have some kind of plan?"

"I'll think of one," Lincoln said, nonplussed.

Mark groaned. "How do we even find these guys?"

At that, Lincoln pulled out his phone. Tapping on it for a few minutes, he held the screen out to Mark.

"According to the Salfran Bay Morgue website, the heads are Arnie Jordan and Grace Myers."

Mark stared at the screen for a moment before it clicked. "The woman called the guy Arnie. You think that was him?"

Lincoln nodded. "Look," Lincoln opened a separate tab on his phone, in which 'Arnie Jordan' was typed into the search bar, and pictures of the man from the morgue lined the screen.

"The other woman was Grace," Lincoln opened up another tab to prove his point.

"I- but... why-"

"Perhaps they were paid to lie about the cause of death," Lincoln mused.

"Yeah... that's gotta be it!" Mark grinned at Lincoln but stopped when he saw his stunned expression.

"Hey, uh... what's-"

"I haven't seen you smile before."

"Oh. Uh..." Mark looked down. "Huh." Mark shrugged, trying to ignore the warmth creeping up in his face.

"I... whatever." Mark looked down at his phone. The clock read 6:30. "Shit. I gotta go home. I told Rick I'd be home at seven."

"That's what you call your father?" Lincoln asked.

Mark glared. "I– he's not my dad. He's just my foster parent."

"Oh." Lincoln looked away from Mark before continuing. "How long have you been living in Salfran Bay?"

"I... since the day before... you know." Mark made an awkward gesture.

"Oh." Lincoln tilted his head down. "That *sucks*."

Mark stared at Lincoln for a long moment. Then, suddenly, he was bursting into uncontrollable laughter.

"Did I say something wrong?"

"No, *no*, it's just..." Mark tried to suppress his laughter. "Yeah. It *does* suck."

"S–U–C–K–S." Mark looked over to Lincoln to find him spelling the word out with a small smile on his face.

"...You know, I haven't seen you smile either," Mark said, smirking.

Lincoln shrugged, still smiling as he looked at the ground. "S-M-I-L-E. S-M-I-L-E. C-H-E-E-S-E."

"God, you're weird," Mark said, grinning.

Suddenly, Lincoln stopped smiling, and the mood in the air shifted.

Mark wondered if he had just put his foot in his mouth. "Uh... I didn't mean it in, like... a bad way."

"People usually mean that in, *like*, a bad way." Lincoln retorted.

The momentary banter was destroyed, and Mark was fully reminded of everything that had happened to him up until this point.

The street was silent for a while before Mark spoke again. "Rick wants me home, remember?" Mark said, a bit too harshly. Turning on his heel, he walked away as quickly as he could.

Alone in his room, for the first time in several days, Mark opened his sketchbook.

Unlike what he had been doing for a while, he didn't try to replicate a scene or an object. He instead drew his emotions from the past few days. He drew the nausea he felt when he found the corpse, the terror when he escaped the burning building, the misery of being called insane.

When Mark was finished, a series of incomprehensible scribbles stared back at him. He crumpled the paper up and threw it across the room, before picking it back up and opening it again, trying to smooth down the paper.

After somewhat salvaging it, he slipped it into the sketchbook and tried to sleep. Yet again, he found that he couldn't.

Mark buried his head against his desk, trying to drown out the sounds of his classmates talking.

He was screwing his eyes shut, trying not to think of the events of the past few days, when he felt a tap on his shoulder. He flinched away, looking up to see Ellie looking at him with concern.

"Hey. Are you good?" She asked, softly.

Mark glared off to the side. "I'm fine. Leave me alone."

"You sure? Cause... not gonna lie, you look like crap."

Mark rolled his eyes. "I *said*, I'm fine."

Ellie sighed. "Look. You don't like me. I get that. But if you need to talk to someone, I... you should. Doesn't have to be me, but still."

Mark stared at Ellie, before looking back down at his desk. "Everything's fine. Really. I... I just... I've been having a shitty week. You *know* that."

Ellie nodded. "Yeah, I... do, I guess." Ellie leaned back in her chair, staring up at the ceiling. "Can't be easy. Moving to a town like this... then... you know."

"Also, I almost got blown up." Mark snorted.

Ellie stared at him for a moment, before laughing. "Welcome to Salfran Bay."

Mark scoffed, and without really thinking, he smiled at Ellie.

"I..." *Fuck it.* "I'm sorry. I was kinda a dick to you before."

"Yep," Ellie replied bluntly.

Mark pursed his lips. "I... I don't really want to make friends. Move around a lot- doesn't really matter."

"Military brat?"

"Foster kid."

"Right."

"And... I didn't wanna talk to you. But I was still a douche. I'm sorry."

Ellie hummed, a smile on her face.

"Apology accepted, *not-friend.*"

Mark chuckled before awkwardly looking away.

"Hey, did you guys hear about the morgue burning down?" A boy in front of him asked his friends.

Mark cringed back into his seat.

Splashing a handful of water into his face, Mark stared into the mirror.

Mark had slipped into the bathroom between classes, and he'd been hiding in there for nearly an hour.

He couldn't take it anymore. He hated being around so many people at once. He didn't know how everyone could sit in a loud, crowded classroom and get shit done without giving their environment a second thought.

He was trying to talk himself into going back to class when he heard footsteps behind him.

"Hey, jackass." Looking into the mirror, Mark stiffened when he saw the boy who was at the lockers the other day.

"Heard about what happened in the woods. Come here to take your meds?"

"I– the hell do you want?" Mark whipped himself around with a snarl.

The boy sneered. "Y'know, I don't think you know who I am." Prowling closer to him, Mark instinctively backed away, his back hitting the sink.

"I'm Axel Warner, and my old man's the mayor here. I can do *whatever* I want around here."

"Oh, great." Mark scoffed. "*Just what the world needs. Another spoiled white boy.*"

Axel's smirk faded, but Mark's momentary satisfaction faded as Axel glared down at him, wrapping his fingers around his throat. "The fuck did you just say to me?"

Before Mark could reply, Axel squeezed down hard. Mark gasped for air, but to no avail. Axel tightened his grip, raising Mark so that his heels were lifted off the ground, and tears involuntarily pricked at his eyes.

And Axel grinned at him the entire time.

Just as Mark's vision was starting to go black, he was let go. Mark hit the ground, gasping.

"Take this as a warning for next time, pretty boy. *Don't. Fuck with me.*" With an almost manic cackle, Axel walked away, leaving Mark to rub at his throat.

Standing, Mark turned to the mirror. Axel had left marks on his neck, but they weren't particularly noticeable. He closed his eyes, trying to calm the throbbing in his skull, the panic twisting in his chest. He shouldn't be overreacting. This wasn't even all that bad. He had dealt with people like Axel before.

He'd live.

Mark walked through the hallways, fully ready to leave the school, before he felt a tap on his shoulder. Flinching, he turned around to see Lincoln, clutching a Post-it note.

"I found out where Arnie Jordan lives," Lincoln whispered, before holding the Post-it out to Mark, continuing in a louder voice. "Meet with me at this address at ten at night tomorrow. Be prepared."

Mark stared at the note, before nodding and slipping it into his pocket. Lincoln kept walking past him.

"Hey."

Mark turned around to face a visibly stunned Ellie.

"Are– are you hanging out with *Lincoln Gray?*" Ellie looked down. "I mean, I don't judge... but you know he's... um..."

"I– yeah." Mark fiddled with the sleeve of his jacket. "It's just– we got a school project."

"A... school project? What class?"

"I... uh... math," Mark said, lamely.

Ellie nodded. "And he wants to meet you... at *ten.*"

"Uh–" Mark shrugged. "I dunno. He's *weird,* remember?"

"I–" Ellie cut herself off. "Cool. Uh, good luck, I guess." Ellie walked away, and Mark let out a long sigh.

"Hey." Mark ran up to Lincoln. "This the house?"

"Yes. Here is a synopsis of the plan. We will put these on so that we are unrecognizable." Lincoln handed Mark a black hoodie and a ski mask. Mark stared at the clothing, before reluctantly shrugging the hoodie on, putting the ski mask over his head. Mark turned to Lincoln, to find him clad in the same outfit.

"Then, we will knock on the door. Then, we will go inside. Then, we will ask him our questions. Then, we will leave." Mark cocked his head. "...okay, but how'd you know he'll talk?"

"Because I have this." Lincoln held something out to him. Mark looked down at it and gasped.

"Where'd you get a *gun*?" Mark hissed.

"My father keeps one in a box in the broom closet," Lincoln replied.

Mark gawked at the pistol. "I– we're not gonna–"

"We will not shoot him, unless in self-defense. This is merely to get him to talk."

"I–" Mark swallowed. "Okay..."

"What the *hell* are you doing?"

Mark whipped his head around, to face Ellie, standing only a few yards away, gaping at the two.

"Ellie?!" Mark hissed. "*What are you doing*– did you *follow us?*"

"*What am I doing?!*" Ellie yelled, running closer to the two. "He's holding a *gun!*"

"Ellie, this isn't–"

"And you guys are dressed like... like– were you gonna *kill* someone?"

"No!" Mark shouted.

"We just wanted to get someone to talk," Lincoln said, holding the gun up.

"*Dude.*" Mark glared at him, before turning back to Ellie. "*Ellie.* We can explain."

"I–" Ellie cut herself off. "You've got five seconds."

"We'd need more than five seconds," Lincoln replied.

"You– *whatever!* Just tell me what the *hell's* going on!"

Lincoln nodded. "Alright– Eric Jacob's death was not a suicide. Mark and I broke into the Salfran Bay Morgue to prove that fact. Then, Arnie Jordan, the man who lives here, along with a woman named Grace Myers, burnt the morgue down. We escaped from the morgue. Now, we are planning on speaking with Arnie to figure out his involvement in the murder."

"...what?" Ellie laughed, turning to Mark. "The hell is he saying?"

"That... that's pretty much it." Mark stared at Lincoln, defeated.

Ellie's smile faded. "...*what?*"

Mark elaborated on their tale, describing everything that had happened to him ever since he found Eric's body.

"...and now, we're gonna talk to Arnie. Figure out what happened."

Ellie stared at Mark with her lips parted."I know, it sounds crazy, but you gotta believe us. I-"

"I... I believe you." Ellie cut him off.

"... Really?" Mark gawked at Ellie. "But... it's-"

"It *does* sound crazy, but... that's the thing." Ellie chuckled hoarsely. "It's too crazy to be a lie."

"I... okay." Mark looked down, before snapping his head back up at Ellie as something occurred to him. "You can't tell *anyone*. About any of this. We could get into some real shit, and I-"

Ellie shook her head. "Don't worry- I won't. Promise."

"...okay." Mark nodded. "Good."

"...But," Ellie stared at Lincoln. "Is the gun really necessary-?"

"Yes." Lincoln said. "Arnie was willing to burn a building down. It will be difficult to get answers out of him, possibly even with the gun. Besides," Lincoln glanced at Mark. "We almost died. Now, he'll feel like he almost died. That is fair."

"I- okay..."

Mark frowned. "Okay, but what are we gonna do about..." He vaguely gestured at Ellie.

"If you're talking about Ellie, she can go home," Lincoln said. "Do not disclose any of this. Now-"

"Wait, *wait*." Ellie cut him off. "I...I wanna help you guys."

"...what?" Mark gaped at Ellie.

"You mean..."Ellie nodded.

"Yeah. This guy..." Ellie glared at the ground.

"If he's just... *running around*, after what he did, I... I can't just... I gotta help catch him."

"Ellie, this... you could get *hurt*," Mark's voice rose at that last word. "I... are you *sure*?"

"I... yeah. I am."

Mark stared at Ellie, before letting out a long sigh. "Okay... what do you think, Lincoln?"

"Three is more than two." He replied.

"Alright... I guess-"

"Four is more than one. Five is more than zero. Six is more than negative one. Seven-"

"*Alright!*" Mark turned to Ellie. "You... you can help us."

Ellie grinned audaciously. "Great."

Despite the fact that Ellie was helping the two out now, she did not have a disguise of her own, and she was forced to stand on the other side of the block, waiting to hear from Mark and Lincoln, who were now on Arnie's front porch.

"Arnie seemed rather meek. There is a chance this will not be difficult." Lincoln turned to Mark. "I still recommend you prepare for the worst-case scenarios."

"Okay..." With a hand that Mark wouldn't have admitted for the world was shaking, he knocked as hard as he could on the door.

After an agonizing few minutes, the door opened. Arnie stood before the two of them, clad in a bathrobe.

"I- who are you-?"

"Arnie Jordan?" Lincoln held the pistol up to his head. "We would like to ask you some questions." Arnie stared at the gun for a long moment, before letting out a squeak that Mark would have laughed at under any other circumstances.

"I– okay! I..." A blanched Arnie backed away. Lincoln and Mark followed him inside, Mark slamming the door behind him.

"W-what are you doing?" Arnie stammered. "I didn't– please don't–!"

"I will not shoot you if you answer our questions truthfully." Lincoln cut him off smoothly, continuing to hold the gun steadily.

"O-*okay*! What do you want–?"

"Why did you and your associate burn down the Salfran Bay Morgue?"

Arnie somehow went a shade paler. "I– *how did you know about that!?*"

"You're not the one asking the questions," Mark said with a snarl.

"I– what do you know?"

"We know that you and Grace Myers burnt the morgue down to cover up the murder of Eric Jacobs. But we would like to know why."

"I–" Arnie gaped stupidly at them. "It was all *Grace's* idea! I didn't–"

"We don't care about that! *Who* made you do that?" Mark took a step forward, standing up as tall as he could in an attempt of intimidation.

It seemed to work, as Arnie visibly shrank. "I– I can't–"

Mark moved closer, and Arnie scrambled back. "*Mayor Warner!* He paid us to do it!"

Mark stopped, as an image of Axel's sadistic grin flashed through his mind.

"The... mayor? *Why?*"

"I... I don't..." Arnie looked away. "Ever since Lila, no one's wanted to come here. Warner didn't like that... he didn't want this town to have another murder on its hands. So... he paid us to say it was suicide. Okay?"

"I...the mayor..." Mark opened and closed his mouth. "Who's Lila?"Arnie stared at him, confused. "You... you don't know?" Lincoln glanced at Mark. "I will explain later." He turned to Arnie. "We've got what we've come for. Tell no one about this."

"Wait... what?" Mark asked, but Lincoln was already halfway out the door. Reluctantly, Mark followed him.

Mark, having enough comprehension of what Arnie had said to feel a spark of anger, turned back just before he left.

"You're a fucking piece of shit." Mark glared at the pathetic man, before slamming the door behind him.

"Wait," Ellie gawked at Mark. "You seriously don't know who Lila was?"

The three, who had come together again, were now sitting in a booth at a hole-in-the-wall diner in the center of town. Save for a group of two or three other customers and a single worker, the diner was empty– understandable, considering how late it was.“*We've covered this.*” Mark rolled his eyes.

Ellie, stunned, laughed a bit. “I– it's just– she's the one thing people know about this town.”

Mark blinked at her. “I... why?”

Okay... I'm gonna admit, this is gonna be kinda rough.” Ellie rubbed her temples, letting out a long sigh before she spoke again.

“About thirty years ago, there was this girl. Lila Carter.” Ellie nodded. “And... no one knew it at the time... but there was this really fucked up cult in town.”

“The People of the Nine Circles, they were called,” Lincoln added, with a hum.

“...Yeah.” Ellie shook her head. “And... they kidnapped Lila. They... they did some really fucked up things to her,” Ellie's voice cracked. “Then... then they killed her.”

Mark didn't have it in him to ask Ellie for details.

“No one knew what happened to her for a month until they found her.” Ellie stared down at the table, scoffing softly. “...Since then, all people know about this town is that a cult tortured and killed a teenaged girl here."

"*Jesus*," Mark whispered.

Then, Lincoln spoke. "The media overtook Salfran Bay. And ever since, Salfran Bay has tried to move past its ruined reputation." Mark caught the way Lincoln's face darkened before he continued. "The city government did this by essentially wiping Lila from the records. In the present, it's a taboo in many circles to even speak of her."

"I–" Mark trailed off, before speaking again. "And now, the mayor's covering up a *fucking murder*." Mark clenched his fists, his knuckles turning white. "He doesn't want Salfran Bay's image to be tarnished again," Lincoln concluded.

"That..." Mark clenched his teeth. "...that *bastard!*" Mark shouted, loudly enough that several customers turned to stare at them. "He thinks he can just... someone was *killed*, for fuck's sake! And I– he–"

"*Mark!*" Ellie yelled, before continuing in a softer voice. "I... I get where you're coming from. I do, but... you need to calm down," she said, gesturing to the people around the diner.

Mark stared at her, before slumping forward. "I–" Mark buried his face in his hands. "He... I thought I was going crazy. No one believed me when I said what I saw. And..." Mark let out a harsh sigh, putting his head back up.

"Mark." Lincoln said softly. Mark looked up, and Lincoln's eyes met his, and he found that there was something undeniable in his normally inexpressive face.

Determination.

"We will find who murdered Eric Jacobs. Then, we will find irrefutable proof that they did so. Then, we will reveal this evidence to the entirety of Salfran Bay. Then, the mayor and all of his associates..." Lincoln shot Mark a small smile. "They'll be subsequently exposed, and dealt their karma."

Mark stared at Lincoln, feeling several conflicting emotions, before he smiled back at him.

"I... are you trying to cheer me up?" Mark asked, a bit incredulous. "Yes, because I do not like seeing other people unhappy. However, this is also the truth."Mark laughed for a bit, before speaking up again. "I... thank you." He said, glancing down at the table."You are welcome." The smile had gradually faded off of Lincoln's face when he finished speaking, and he said this with the neutral expression that Mark was used to seeing.

"No. Not just for that just now– thank you, for... for *everything*." Mark felt his face warm, and he wrung his hands together. "I... you believed me when no one else did. And... I'll admit, you do some really weird shit, I'm not saying you don't, but... you helped me a lot through everything. I know I haven't been the nicest to you, and I'm sorry, but... thank you."

Mark looked up at Lincoln, and he had a comical expression on his face, his eyebrows almost seeming to rise past his hairline.

"...Again, you are welcome," Lincoln said, a small smile crossing his face once again. Mark couldn't help but grin back at him.

After a few moments, Ellie loudly cleared her throat. "Sorry to... *interrupt*, or whatever... but what do we do now?"

"We..." Mark's face crumbled. "We're back at square one. The Mayor might've covered it up, but we still don't know who actually did it."

"We can go to the forest tomorrow. Investigate." Lincoln suggested. "That was the other idea."

"Other ide– oh." Mark chuckled, remembering his earlier conversation with Lincoln. Ellie looked at the two strangely.

"Okay. We'll go tomorrow, right after school." Mark glanced between Ellie and Lincoln. "Can you two make it?"

The two nodded in unison.

"Okay. I'll see you then." Mark got up and left the diner, with a lightness that he hadn't felt in a while.

"*Fuck.*" Mark kicked an old tree stump as if to emphasize his words.

"Language." Ellie tutted, though Mark saw the frown on her face.

Lincoln was crouching on the ground, ripping a dead leaf into pieces. "Perhaps this was to be expected," Lincoln took a scrap of the leaf and sniffed at it, before scattering the bits and pieces of the leaf on the ground. "Coverup or not, the police would have cleaned this area up thoroughly."

Their hours of poking around the crime scene had come to no avail, and none of them knew any more than they did when they started.

Throwing his hands up, Mark dropped himself down onto the stump, crouching on its edge.

"So... that's it. We're screwed again, huh?"

"Hey, chin up." Ellie took a few steps closer to Mark. "Maybe we're missing something. We can come back tomorrow. If we still can't come up with anything, we'll figure something out."

Mark shrugged, not looking up at Ellie.

Lincoln glanced up at the sky. "The sun is setting. We should regroup tomorrow." With that, the trio left the forest and went their separate ways.

Mark was soon left to his own thoughts as he began to walk back. Despite everything that had happened, Mark still felt the same twisted curiosity he had felt ever since Ellie had revealed the crime Salfran Bay was infamous for.

When he arrived back at Rick's house, Mark made a beeline for his room, pulling out his cell phone as he collapsed on the bed.

He stared at his phone for what could have been any time frame from a minute to an hour, before opening Google.

With a quickened heartbeat, he typed '*lila carter death*'.

He was immediately met with a series of oversaturated images of a messy-haired, round-faced girl grinning widely at the camera, which only served to highlight the gap between her front teeth.

It was clear that she was younger than Mark– he put her at around thirteen or fourteen.

Mark felt his throat involuntarily tighten.

He scrolled through a series of poorly placed ads before finally clicking on a potentially credible website.

It was a news article with yet another picture of Lila plastered under its title– '*Remembering Lila Carter.*'

Reluctantly scrolling down, Mark froze when he read the first sentence of the report.

Ellie had said that the murder had occurred *'about thirty years ago,'* not *'almost exactly thirty years ago today.'*

And yet, the date detailed in the article stated that it had– thirty years ago, not even two weeks back.

Mark stared at the date for a long moment, before continuing to scroll through the report.

The more he read, the sicker Mark felt as he gradually realized that Ellie had horrifically understated what the cult had done to Lila.

Not having it in him to read the full report, he scrolled to the end to find that, when Lila's body was recovered, it was beyond recognition.

The entire cult was killed in the resulting shootout.

The next day was just as unsuccessful as the last.

The three went to the diner that they had come to the other night, even sitting in the same booth. But now, as it was relatively early in the evening, the diner was far more active, the air flooding with idle chatter.

"Y'know, my parents are pretty rich," Ellie said. "I... I really don't wanna do this, but maybe I could take some money from them. Pay off a P.I."

"I..." Mark slumped over. "Sounds like a longshot, but I can't think of anything else."

"Mull over it. If we are truly bereft of other options, do so." Lincoln said. After a brief pause, he continued. "We should exchange numbers."

Mark blinked. "Oh. You mean..." Mark pulled out his phone.

"It'll make communications more efficient," Lincoln said, taking out his own phone. Ellie nodded and took her phone out.

"You can just put your number into mine," Mark said, handing his phone to Lincoln.

Lincoln nodded but stopped when he glanced at Mark's phone screen.

Mark frowned. "What–"

"You were reading a Lila Carter article." Mark flinched. "How–?" Mark leaned over the table, to glance at his phone.

He had never closed out of the article from the other day.

"Uh... that was just..." Mark quickly took his phone back, closing out of the article.

"There's nothing wrong with that."

"Yeah, I *know* there isn't," Mark said, scoffing. "I... it's just that..."

"You... wanted to know more?" Ellie added. When Mark didn't respond, Ellie continued. "It's no big deal. A year ago, I was really into those true-crime podcasts. Is... is it like that?"

"...yeah. Kinda." Mark wrung his hands together.

"...You know, at the town library, they have these books in the back closet." Ellie glanced at Mark. "Rare books. A lot of them are just some random first editions, but... they actually have some books about Lila. And the cult. Like, first-hand accounts of everything."

"...Really?" Mark frowned at Ellie.

"Yeah. I think the librarian will let you look at them if you want."

"...huh." Mark glanced up at the ceiling.

"...gotta go. Rick wants me home." With a grunt, Mark stood and walked out of the diner.

Mark was back to sitting at his isolated table in the cafeteria, trying to ignore the sounds and chatter that came with every high school cafeteria. He picked at his pizza, which defied the rule that all pizza, even bad pizza, was tasty.

Across the cafeteria, he watched Ellie, sitting at a ridiculously overcrowded table, laughing and chatting with several girls at once.

He wondered how she did it. Just the thought of sitting with that many people made Mark feel nauseous.

"Hello, Mark." Mark flinched and whipped himself around to face Lincoln.

"*Stop doing that.* You scared the fuck out of me."

"That wasn't my intention. I won't do it again." Lincoln sat down next to Mark.

"...did you find something?" Mark asked, hushed.

Lincoln shook his head.

Mark frowned. "I... then why are you here?"

"I felt like sitting here. If you don't, I'll find somewhere else."

"I–" Mark pursed his lips. "I... guess it's fine."

Lincoln hummed, before pulling out his lunchbox. Clicking it open, he pulled out a small, plastic tray, with little pockets in them filled with food.

"I– is that–?" Mark gawked at Lincoln's Lunch. Squinting at it, he confirmed that, in fact, it was a YummieLunchie– a premade, store-bought meal, famously made for small children five and under.

"Dude, that shit's for *kids*." Mark blurted.

"I'm aware. My parents are under the impression that I'm ten years younger than I actually am." Peeling the plastic off the tray, Lincoln rolled a small cube of cheese between his fingers.

Mark snorted. "For real?"

"No. They are aware that I'm seventeen. I was using hyperbole to express my irritation that they treat me like a child."

"Not what I meant," Mark grumbled before Lincoln's words had sunk in. "Oh. Uh...they do?" Mark asked, dumbly.Lincoln popped the cheese into his mouth. "Yes."

Mark pursed his lips. "I... that sucks, man."

"S-U-C-K-S." Lincoln replied.

Mark snorted. "I'm serious, dude. If you're seventeen and they're packing you... *this*," Mark vaguely gestured at the tray. "That... that sucks."

"It does." Lincoln glanced down at the floor.A long moment of silence ensued, and Mark was just starting to come up with an excuse to leave the table before a question that'd been on his mind before popped into his head again.

"Hey, man... I gotta ask." Mark, nervously, scratched at the back of his neck. "Like I said, I... I appreciate it and all, but... why'd you help me?" Lincoln stopped eating and stared down at his lunch. "Please elaborate. I'm confused."

"I mean, *everyone* in town thought I was lying but you. You didn't have any real reason to believe me, right? So... why...?"

"Did I help you?" Lincoln finished for him. Wringing his hands together, he answered.

"Because the first day we met, you protected me from Axel Warner. So you had to be good, so you deserved to be helped."It took a moment to decipher Lincoln's words.

"I... that's it?" Mark asked, dumbly. "But... I could've been lying."

"Like I said, you're good. So you likely weren't lying."

"I could've been *seeing shit*."

"Like I said, you're good. So even if you were, you deserved to be helped through it."

"You–" Mark cut himself off. "I– I tried to pick a fight with some asshole, and that's all it took?"

"Yes."

"I–" Mark stared at Lincoln. "You– you're insane." When Lincoln tensed, Mark continued. "*Thank you.*"

Slowly, Lincoln relaxed and turned to Mark. "You're welcome." He replied, with a small smile on his face.

After a long moment, Mark tried to break the silence. "You know, maybe it's best you stick with that," Mark pointed at the YummieLunchie with a chuckle. "School lunch here is shit."

"A traditional description for a high school lunch," Lincoln said, still smiling. "However, it's not *shit*– it's dough, tomato sauce, and cheese."

"Yep. Shit probably tastes better." Mark snorted.

"That is surely an exaggeration."

"Nope." Mark tore a small piece of the crust off. "Try it."

Lincoln told the piece and popped it into his mouth. "I stand corrected." He said, with a smile.

Their banter continued to the end of lunch, marked by the sound of a bell ringing. With a slight wave, Mark trashed his lunch and walked away.

Looking at his phone, Mark confirmed that he was in the right place.

The Salfran Bay Library was a relatively small building stationed at the edge of town, several blocks away from the nearest house. Mark was forced to walk for nearly two hours before he arrived.

After hesitating for a bit, Mark walked inside, with a bell on the glass door ringing.

"Oh! Hello there!" Mark turned to his left to face an old lady with short, curly white hair, sitting at a desk, giving him a wide smile. "Could I help you?"

"Uh... yeah. Can I check out the... rare books?" The elderly woman made an 'o' with her mouth, before grinning even wider and clapping her hands together. "Of course! Just behind the shelf in the back."

Mark grunted a 'thank you' and made his way around the library, which was crowded with bookshelves.

He found the room, with a sign reading 'RARE BOOKS' hung over the top of it. He opened the door and stepped inside.

The 'room' turned out to be so small, that Mark legitimately suspected that it was a repurposed broom closet. There was a single metal shelf placed against the back wall, lined with thick, old books.

Closing the door behind him, Mark took a step toward the shelf. He ran his hands over the various titles, most meaning nothing to him, before he found one that made him take a sharp breath.

'THE MANIFESTO OF THE PEOPLE OF THE NINE CIRCLES'

With a trembling hand, Mark pulled the book out of the shelf, laying it out on the ground. Sitting down, he cracked it open, the book opening to a page in the middle.

'The creation of demonic entities has always pleased our Lord Satan. As further detailed on page 42, the conventional way of doing so is a simple human sacrifice, complete with a demonification ritual. However, we have heard talk of a method that could allow us to create an extremely powerful entity, nearly as powerful as his majesty himself, called an Azrog.'

To create an Azrog, a human virgin must be subjected to the torture detailed on the next few pages for six hundred and sixty-six hours— not a second less, without any stop. Immediately after, the virgin must be killed.

Then, for thirty years, we would have to sit and wait. But on the anniversary of their death, the following incantation would have to be read—

"I vow to every demon in hell, and upon Satan himself,

I devote myself to thee, you future Azrog."

The Azrog will then become an extremely powerful being, capable of completely destroying the world...*'

At that, Mark slammed the book closed, overcome by nausea and outrage.

A young girl, put through hell for the sake of a delusion.

He stood, prepared to leave the library, and never come back, when curiosity overtook him yet again.

That last word had an asterisk. Mark wanted to know what it was linked to.

Slowly, Mark crouched back onto the ground and flipped to the end of the chapter.

'*Please note that this is assuming that the performer of the incantation has enacted at least three human sacrifices, as is standard for a Person of the Nine. If not, it is rumored that after the summoning, the potential Azrog would be forced to possess the performer for the last quarter of the day, every quarter moon.'

Scoffing, Mark closed the book again, standing up to leave, when a realization stopped him dead in his tracks.

A quarter moon was a week.

The week after the anniversary of Lila Carter's murder was the death of Eric Jacobs.

"It's a coincidence, right? Has to be." Mark drummed his fingers against the corner of the page.

Ellie frowned. "I– that doesn't..."

"If it's a mere coincidence, why did you call us so late?" Lincoln stared down at the book laid out on the table.

"I– maybe there's some... connection?" Mark asked. "I mean, demons aren't real. Obviously. I'm not fucking stupid. But... maybe the cult had something to do with this?"

"Everyone in the cult at the time of Lila's death is dead. But perhaps someone attempted to summon an Azrog and nearly succeeded."

Mark scoffed. "You– you can't be serious."

"You find this hard to believe. But don't you also find it hard to believe that these instructions line up perfectly with what's been happening, purely by coincidence?"

"I– like I said, the cult might have something to do with this. Doesn't mean there's fucking *demons*–"

"Guys, stop." Ellie interrupted. "Okay, Mark might be right. The cult might've done *something*, but that doesn't really mean there *are* demons."

"Thank you," Mark grumbled, but Ellie cut him off with a sharp glance.

"But... it's not like any of us have proof that demons *don't* exist." Ellie squeezed the bridge of her nose for a moment, before letting out a long sigh. "I guess... we should... keep an open mind."

Mark stared at Ellie, before scoffing softly. "Okay. Whatever. But what do we do now?"

"We should do further research on the People of the Nine," Lincoln said, playing with a lock of his hair with both his hands.

Mark frowned. "When you say research, do you mean, like, internet, or–?"

"The library," Lincoln replied, still playing with his hair.

Mark groaned.

The door's bell chimed as Mark, Lincoln, and Ellie walked inside.

"Hey, we were just gonna poke around and–" Mark stopped, when he got a good look at the old librarian– and noticed the obviously unsettled expression on her face.

"Are you alright?" Mark asked, feeling a prick of concern.

"Oh, yes, yes, I'm alright." The librarian smiled, but Mark could easily see that it was strained. "It's just... ah..." As if on cue, a towering figure came out from behind the shelves, walking up to the trio.

Mark tensed when he recognized him.

"Axel?" Ellie glared. "What are you doing here?"

Axel raised an eyebrow, letting out a laugh. "It's a free town, jackass." Axel took a step closer to them, and Mark had to tell himself to stay still.

Ellie shook her head. "Look. We don't want any trouble. Just... get out of the way and–"

"And what?" Axel sneered, crouching down a bit to smirk at Ellie. His smirk grew when Ellie stayed quiet. "C'mon. You were so feisty a minute ago."

"*Fuck off,*" Mark snarled.

Axel's face darkened, and Mark willed himself not to break eye contact with him.

After what felt like an eternity, Axel scoffed, shaking his head. He pushed past Mark, deliberately bumping into him hard enough that he stumbled for a bit.

Mark didn't look back, but hearing the door's bell chime, he knew that Axel had left.

"I... I'm so sorry." The librarian shook her head. "If he..." She trailed off, and all Mark could do was nod at her, before the trio wordlessly hurried to the back room.

"I take it you ran into Axel before?" Ellie asked as she leaned against the wall.

"Yep." Mark shook his head.

Lincoln hummed, sitting on the floor with his legs crossed. "The apple did not fall far from the tree. The Axel did not fall far from the tree." Lincoln paused briefly. "The tree is the mayor."

"Yeah, I got that," Mark grumbled.

"God, I hate that psycho." Ellie glared at the ground. "That poor lady... he *better* not hurt her."

"...you know, he tried to choke me out the other day. See?" Mark tilted his head up, pushing his hair back.

"What?" Ellie quickly turned to look at his neck. Mark knew that while the bruises were faded, they *could* be seen.

"Oh, *God*. Mark," Ellie shook her head, giving Mark a pitying look.

Mark looked away. "It's not like he was gonna kill me. He let me go."

"It's still a cause for concern." Mark looked down at Lincoln, who had just spoken. He was still staring down at the floor, but he could see how his brows were furrowed. "You could have been seriously hurt."

"Yeah, I *know that.*" Mark snorted. "But, it wasn't *that* bad." Absently, Mark rubbed his fingers over his neck. "One time, one of my old foster dads got so drunk, he *actually* tried to strangle me. Had to go to the ER." He let out a hoarse laugh, finding he had to force it out.

Ellie stared at him in horror. "...*What?* Really? That–That's *horrible.* I... I'm so sorry."

"It's in the past." Mark shrugged, with a casualness he didn't feel. "Rick's... honestly, pretty good. I... don't really have to worry about that stuff anymore."

Ellie stopped for a moment before she looked away. "Okay... we– we should probably start looking around."

The room was silent for a while, save for an occasional question and answer. The three shuffled through the shelves, taking out any books that had some relevance to Lila's death and placing them in a pile on the floor.

After Lincoln put one last book down, he spoke. "When I was nine years old, a girl hit my head with a brick. She did so very hard. The doctors said it was a miracle I didn't sustain any permanent brain damage."

Mark and Ellie stopped to stare at him.

"I... god," Ellie said, hoarsely.

Mark felt a strange appreciation for Lincoln's words at that moment.

After a brief moment of silence, they sat on the ground and started flipping through the books. The room was quiet for about ten minutes before Ellie spoke up.

"Guys, I got something!" Mark and Lincoln both peeked over Ellie's shoulder.

"*The People of the Nine were said to have obtained their knowledge of demons and the occult from a woman named Alita Estia. Estia claimed she was a seer who had frequent visions relating to the occult and spread them via word of mouth. Ever since the crimes of The People of the Nine were brought to the public eye, she has essentially faded off the grid.*"Ellie read this aloud as Mark followed the words on the page.

"She could just be crazy." Mark drawled after the three all went quiet for a bit.

Lincoln cleared his throat. "If we speak to her, it's possible that we can confirm if she was telling the truth about her visions or not– and by extension, if there is, in fact, a demon in Salfran Bay."

"But... how would we find her?" Ellie asked.

Lincoln smiled. "Utilizing the internet, I will do so tonight."

"Where were you?" Rick glared, crossing his arms.

"Out." Mark said, closing the door behind him. "It's *nine*. I told you to get back at seven."

Mark shrugged, trying to walk past him.

"*Hey*," Rick grasped his shoulder, stopping him in place. "We need to talk."

Mark stared at Rick, before sighing and nodding.

Rick directed Mark to the couch. Sitting down beside him, Rick frowned down at him.

"First, where were you?"

"...The library. I was studying with a couple of my classmates." It technically wasn't a lie, but Mark still shifted in his seat.

"Until *nine*?" Rick snorted.

"We lost track of time. I didn't think it was a big deal."

"Okay. But... kid. Are you okay?"

Mark wasn't sure of what he expected to hear next, but it wasn't that.

"Yeah...? I'm fine–"

"Look, I haven't really been paying attention to you. I'm sorry about that." Rick pursed his lips before he continued. "But I *care*. I know, you've had a rough time, because of... you know, and I'm kinda worried about you." Mark cocked his head at Rick. "It's... I'm fine. Thanks, for... asking."

"...Are you sure?

Mark nodded.

"Okay. Yeah. Yeah, that's good." Rick stood up, stretching a bit. "I... get some sleep tonight, okay?" With that, he walked off.

Mark stared at him as he walked away, completely baffled.

A couple of hours later, Lincoln had texted him.

Lincoln: *I found out where Alita Estia lives.*

*Here is the address:*Lincoln then sent a Google Maps link. Mark gawked at the address.

Mark: *riverview? thats 4 hours by car, tf*

Lincoln: *So you have other leads. Rest assured, you are welcome to share them.*

Mark: *fuck you.*

Lincoln: *That is not a lead.*

Mark snorted.

Mark: *seriously, how would we get there?*

Lincoln: *I already texted Ellie. She has a license and a car.*

Lincoln: *We plan to leave tomorrow after school. Come up with an alibi for then.*

Mark paused for a bit before he replied.

Mark: *okay.*

Mark: *a brick, huh*

Mark immediately cringed at that last text, wondering if it was possible to delete it before Lincoln replied.

Lincoln: *If you're referring to what I mentioned in the library, yes. I was hit on the head with a brick when I was nine years old.*

Mark: *jesus. what happened*

Mark paused, before quickly typing out something else.

Mark: *if you don't mind*

Lincoln: *When I was a small child, I acted in strange ways. As such, the other kids thought it was okay to hurt me.*

Lincoln: *I was beaten a lot.*

Lincoln: *I tried to act 'normal' sometimes, to make it stop. But it made me tired. And it hurt. And it never even worked. Then I stopped acting. Then came the girl with the brick.*

Mark: *did you even do anything to her*

Lincoln: *I actually did, by accident.*

Lincoln: I told her her dress was ugly, because I didn't know talking about a dress would hurt her feelings. It wasn't like she made it.

Lincoln: At least I took away a valuable lesson about honesty.

Mark: god

Mark: im sorry

Lincoln: You didn't hit me.

Mark: i know. your just supposed to say that.

Mark: i know that kind of stuffs annoying. ill take it back.

Lincoln: I like the sentiment, though.

Lincoln: Since I talked about my near-death experience, can we talk about yours?

Mark: oh

Mark: yeah, my foster parents were drunk assholes 99% of the time.

Mark: just wanted money from the state

Lincoln: $_$

Mark: ...you deserved to be bullied

Mark: lincoln?

Mark: i was kidding. sorry. that was fucked up.

Lincoln: I thought you were, but I wasn't sure. It's okay.

Mark: Okay.

Lincoln: I'm sorry, too.

Mark: *for what*

Lincoln: *That's what you're supposed to say.*

Mark: Oh.

Mark: *shit.*

Putting his phone down for a moment, Mark began laughing uncontrollably, with an audible hint of hysteria.

Mark: *you're right*

Lincoln: *I am, more often than not.*

Lincoln: *Are we friends, Mark?*

Mark blinked at the screen, stilling for a long moment before he replied.

Mark: *where'd that come from*

Lincoln: *If you're talking about the question, it came from you sharing something from your past.*

Lincoln: *I'm not sure, but I don't think you're supposed to share that with people who aren't your friends.*

Mark stared at the screen for a long time, as a series of memories clouded his mind.

When Mark was thirteen, he had been placed in a particularly awful home. He was forced to steal most of his food, and he had to sleep outside on more than one occasion.

But at the school there, he had met Jason, Phoebe, and John.

They'd taken Mark under their wing. They'd play video games at Jason's house. They'd draw graffiti on the school walls. They'd give Mark a shoulder to cry on, and they snuck him snacks whenever they could.

Mark hadn't had friends since he was a little kid. And yet, those three had come into his life, and given him something to care about in that hellhole of a city.

When Mark had to move again, they'd tearfully hugged him goodbye, promising that they'd call and text him all the time.

When he arrived at the new home, they were initially texting constantly, Mark updating them on practically everything that happened to him.

Then, their long conversations faded into curt, one-word replies.

Then, after a month of unread calls and texts, they all blocked him at once.

Mark didn't try to make friends anymore after that.

Mark: *you wanna be my friend?*
Lincoln: *Yes.*
Mark: *i keep treating you like shit though*
Lincoln: *I told you– you are a good person.*

Lincoln: *And you haven't flushed me down any toilets.*

Mark bit his lip. He remembered the hours he'd spent crying when his friends had cut him off, how he'd seriously wondered if he'd be better off dead, how he'd stopped eating for a week, even when the hunger crippled him.

But he also remembered the various back-and-forths he'd shared with Lincoln, how he had believed him against all odds, how he had lent an ear to the things that he said.

Feeling a bit impulsive, Mark typed out a response.

Mark: *okay. i guess we can be.*

Lincoln: *Okay. We are friends now– confirm this.*

Mark: *...we are*

Lincoln: *Good. I look forward to seeing our relationship develop.*

Snickering at his phone, Mark texted Lincoln one last time, before curling up into bed.

Mark: *me too, i guess. gn*

Lincoln: *Good night.*

"So. Today, after school, right?" Ellie asked as she sat herself down at her desk.

Mark nodded at Ellie. "Yeah. I'll text Rick that I'm staying over at a friend's. Can we meet in the school parking lot?"

Ellie nodded. "Yep! And I'll tell my folks I'm at Kelsey's for the night. Got her to cover for me." She stopped smiling, furrowing her brows. "Only problem is that she won't stop asking me about 'who the guy is.'"

Mark snorted. "It's two guys, actually."

Ellie snickered. "If I told her that, that'd make things worse."

"It's the truth."

"Yeah, but I'm like... 99% sure you two would be more into *each other* than me, so..." When Mark gaped at her, she threw her hands up. "I'm kidding! I'm kidding. Besides, neither of you are really my type."

"...What *is* your type?" Mark asked, cocking an eyebrow.

Ellie put her index finger in front of her lips, making a shushing gesture. "It's a secret."

Mark smirked wryly. "Okay..."

"What're *you* doing?"

A girl with bleached blonde hair strutted up to the two.

"I–" Ellie glanced at Mark. "Just talking."

The girl sneered down at him. "With *this* psycho? C'mon Ellie, you know what he did."

Mark clenched his jaw, glaring down at his desk.

"He was *panicking.* You know that!"

The girl rolled her eyes. "Sure. Panicking."

"Just because you can't spell it doesn't mean it isn't true." Mark said with a snort.

The girl's face turned the color of pepperoni. "Oh, screw you, you– you freak!"

Mark hated the way that the childish insult manage to induce a pang in his stomach.

Shaking her head, the girl recollected herself. "Whatever. It's your funeral." She strutted away, her high heels clicking against the ground.

As the girl sat herself at the front of the room, Ellie turned to Mark. "I... I'm sorry about her."

Mark shook his head. "It's fine." Leaning back in his seat, he glanced at Ellie. "What's her deal, anyway?"

"She's... in my friend group, I guess. But we're not really *friends...* I–" Ellie pursed her lips. "She comes to my parties sometimes, and we sit near each other at lunch. But that's it. She's... she's not *always* like that."

Mark turned away from Ellie to stare out the window.

"Hey." Mark shot a slight wave at Lincoln.

"Hello, Mark." Lincoln smiled, patting the seat next to him.

Mark sat next to Lincoln, putting his tray down at the table. "Okay, so Ellie said we're gonna meet up in the parking lot." He said, absently twisting his pathetic excuse for spaghetti with a plastic fork.

"That's acceptable." Lincoln took his lunchbox out, and sure enough, there was another YummieLunchie in it.

"Chicken nuggets, huh?" Mark snickered, glancing at the poorly defrosted food.

"Would you be willing to trade lunches?" Lincoln asked, looking at his lunch distastefully.

"Oh, fuck *yeah*." Mark immediately switched the trays around, gnawing at the low-grade chicken that still managed to be an upgrade from the cafeteria food.

As soon as Lincoln took a good look at the pasta, his face scrunched up. "Would you be willing to trade lunches?"

"No," Mark replied with a cackle.

"Please? Please? Please? Please–"

"You made a bad choice, man. Not my problem."

Lincoln was silent for a bit before he spoke again. "Alright. I accept the consequences of my actions."

Mark laughed, before lowering his voice. "So... how much could you find on Alita?"

"She lives in Riverview, in an apartment building on Trinity Road. She is most likely in her sixties. That is it."

Mark pursed his lips, before staring down at the table. "Guess we gotta figure out the rest from there."

"Well, well, well. Look at that. Figures, you two would be all buddy buddy." Mark flinched, turning to face Axel, who was crossing his arms, a smirk on his face.

"You homos gonna shoot up the school together?" Axel sneered, taking a seat next to Mark. He instinctively scooted away.

"First of all, that is homophobic. Second of all, we have no intention of committing a school shooting. Third of all, please leave us alone."

Axel cackled. "I'll do whatever I want. Maybe you can go cry to mommy about it, you retarded fucking baby."

Lincoln then said something about ableism, and Axel said something scathing in response, but Mark was too lost in his thoughts to truly listen.

Axel was right. He could do whatever he wanted. And for the first time, it fully registered in Mark's head why that was.

Axel's dad was the mayor– a man willing to cover up a murder for no reason other than to protect the town's reputation. Of course, he would do the same with Axel's actions.

Axel could get away with practically anything, all because of the endorsement of a sociopath that made him question his own sanity, that almost got him killed, that forced him to involve himself in a horrific crime.

At that last thought, without thinking, Mark clenched his fist, and drove it as hard as he could into the side of Axel's face. Axel's body slammed into the side of the table, and he slowly bought a hand up to his cheek. Then, he was snarling, and the next thing he knew, Mark was on the ground, Axel gripping his throat. Mark was vaguely aware of people yelling at them as he kicked at him as hard as he could, gritting his teeth through the pain. Then, he and Axel were pulled away from one another and were both dragged away.

"Okay." Ms. Muff said with a sigh, cupping her mouth in her hands. "It's come to my attention that there was an... *incident* between the two of you." She said, looking at Axel and Mark. "And you," She then turned to Lincoln, "were a direct witness to what had happened."

"He *fucking* hit me," Axel growled. Mark rolled his eyes.

"Ms. Muff, I would like to point out that, while Mark did hit Axel, it was in response to him harassing us."

Ms. Muff shook her head. "That is no excuse to assault another student. However," Ms. Muff frowned at Axel. "There was no need to respond the way you did, Axel. Mark could have been seriously hurt."

Axel scoffed in response.

"So," Ms. Muff nodded at the two. "I am giving both of you an hour of detention after school."

"...*That's it?*" Mark gawked at Ms. Muff. The last fight he had gotten into at school, he'd been suspended for a week.

"Yes. If one or both of you do not show up, I will have to issue a more severe punishment." Ms. Muff said, scribbling on two pink slips, handing one each to Axel and Mark.

"Alright. The three of you are dismissed."

As the three left the room, Axel smirked at Mark as he walked away.

Mark glared after him. "An *hour*." He snarled, clenching his fists. "He had his hands around my *fucking neck*, in front of *everyone*, and he only got an hour."

Lincoln pursed his lips, not looking at him. "That is bad. But it is good that you only got an hour as well."

Mark sighed. "I guess we're gonna have to go a little later." Then, realizing something, Mark stopped for a moment. "Fuck. Rick's gonna be pissed." He turned to Lincoln, worried.

"Do you think he's gonna keep me at the house?"

"Perhaps," Lincoln replied, bluntly. "Why did you do that?" He asked, saying it more like a statement than a question.

"You mean..." Mark made a fist, haphazardly miming a punch. Lincoln nodded.

"I...what his dad did... it just– it popped into my head, and I... I was so *mad*."

Lincoln simply hummed in response.

"I–I'm sorry if I screwed things up. It–"

"It's alright." Lincoln cut him off.

Mark blinked. "I– for real?"

"Yes. We can figure something out, in the worst-case scenario. Besides…" Lincoln grinned and made eye contact with him. "It was satisfying, watching that son of a bitch get punched."

Mark stared at Lincoln before he began to laugh uncontrollably.

"What? He is, in fact, a son of a bitch. At least, in the metaphorical sense. Why–"

"No, no, you're right, you're right." Mark wiped his eyes, which had tears in them. "It's just… you. Cursing."

"Oh." Lincoln raised an eyebrow. "Is me cursing amusing to you?"

"I–kinda!"

Lincoln paused for a long moment. Just as Mark was starting to worry if he had said something wrong, Lincoln spoke again.

"Bitch. Crap. Fuck. Hell."

Mark gaped at him. And then he began to laugh again. "Damn. Shit. Cu–"

"Stop." Mark cut him off, still cackling.

"Alright."

Mark stopped laughing, and the two stood in silence for a moment.

"You know, I'm glad we're friends," Mark said.

Lincoln raised an eyebrow.

Mark looked away. "Uh... sorry if that's–"

"So am I."

Mark turned to Lincoln, who met his eyes, smiling at him.

Albeit with a bit of hesitance, Mark smiled back.

Once again, the car ride home was silent but tense.

Mark was half-hoping that the silence between the two of them would continue forever, but it didn't.

"Kid. We gotta talk." Rick said, once they walked inside.

Mark followed Rick to the dining table, sitting across from him.

"Look, I'm sorry. I know, I shouldn't have–"

"I'm not mad, kid."

Mark looked up at Rick in shock.

"Look, everyone in town knows that kid's a sociopath. I don't know what happened back there, but whatever it was, I know you probably had a good reason to do what you did."

Mark raised an eyebrow. "So... I'm *not* in trouble?" Mark asked, hopefully.

His hopes crumbled when Rick furrowed his brows.

"No. But there's... there's something we have to talk about."

Mark frowned. "...okay...what?"

Rick pursed his lips, taking in a long breath before he replied.

"You don't want to talk to me. I get that. But..." He paused, pinching the bridge of his nose. "Kid, I'm not stupid. I know that there's been *something* going on with you, ever since you... you found that guy."

"I–" Mark narrowed his eyes. "What are you talking about?"

"...I think you need to talk to someone. A therapist."

Mark stared at Rick for a long moment.

"...Therapy? What– no– I... what?"

"Mark." Rick cut him off. "I know you had a tough life. And ever since you... you know, you've been acting... strange. I know you're going through something, and you need help. Like I said, you don't have to talk to me, but... you have to talk to someone. So..."

Rick continued, but Mark couldn't hear him.

The moment Rick bought up therapy, Mark's thoughts were drowned out by memories of being force-fed pills, men with clipboards telling him awful things while he cried, men and women screaming about how insane he was, being unable to say anything in response without making things worse.

"...Mark–?"

"I– I don't need *therapy*." Mark sprung up from the table. "I– I *don't*. I'm not *crazy*. *I'm not!*"

Rick shook his head. "You're not. No one's saying that. You you just need–"

"*I'm fine!*" Mark spat. "I– I am. I..."

Mark stared down at himself. "I... I gotta go. To my friend's house, remember?"

Mark hurried out of the house. He heard Rick yell, but he slammed the door shut behind him.

Mark didn't know how long he was running before he finally sat down at a park bench.

Rick thought he was crazy. That was the only explanation for what he had said.

"I'm not crazy. *I'm not.*" Mark muttered.

But in the back of his head, there was a voice screaming that he was. That all of his doctors, his foster parents, were right. He was just some psychopath who needed to be drugged up to be anything close to a normal person. He was weak, and worthless, and had to have others take care of him and his problems like he wasn't seventeen.

Curling up into the bench, he screwed his eyes shut, trying to drown the voice out, to no avail.

After a few minutes, he stood. He still felt terrible, but his earlier feelings had abated somewhat.

Now, Mark was left embarrassed. What had come over him? Why did he have to overreact like that?

He vowed to tell Rick he was sorry when he got home, and suck it up and do the therapy crap he'd suggested.

But first, he had to go find Ellie and Lincoln.

Following the address Ellie had sent him on Google Maps, he arrived at a mall parking lot in the center of town.

He looked around for a bit before he heard the honk of a horn.

"Get in, loser!" Ellie yelled through a rolled-down window, grinning.

Mark felt himself smile as he walked over to her car.

"To clarify– Ellie does not genuinely think you are a loser. Her referring to you as such was a reference to a movie."

"Yeah. I got that." Mark slipped into the passenger seat of Ellie's car, slamming th door shut. "Why'd you have a car like this, Ellie?" He asked her, cocking an eyebrow.

Ellie grinned. "Rich parents, remember?"

The car, in question, was a gorgeous silver BMW that, judging from the way it had gleamed in the sunset, had come fresh out of the factory.

Mark snorted. "I don't care *how* rich you are, you don't give a seventeen-year-old a BMW. You got your license, what, last year?"

"This year, actually. I had to put off taking the classes."

"Proving my point."

"Anyway!" Ellie clapped her hands together. "I found the *perfect* playlist."

Ellie shoved her phone into Mark's face. He squinted at the Spotify playlist she had opened.

"*POV: You're going on a road trip to confront someone in order to try and solve a murder mystery.*" Mark read aloud, stunned. "That's... specific."

Ellie giggled and slammed the phone into the speaker.

At some point, Lincoln had fallen asleep. Mark tried not to laugh at his comically loud snoring.

"Hey, Mark?"

Mark glanced at Ellie, whose eyes were still on the road. "Yeah?"

"Can I ask you something?"

"...sure?"

"Are you okay?"

Mark frowned. "What...? What do you mean–"

"You seem fine now... but when you got to the car, you– I could've been seeing things, but... it kinda looked like you were crying." Mark winced. *Fuck.*

"Oh, uh... I have allergies. Around this time of year. And my eyes get red, so..."

"Oh." Ellie raised her eyebrow. "That's all that was?"

"...yeah."

"...Okay. That's good." Ellie nodded, but looking at her face, Mark couldn't tell if she was convinced.

Save for Lincoln's snoring, the car was silent for a minute before Ellie spoke again.

"Hey, Mark? If... you know, you were *actually* crying– I know you weren't, but if you were– you can vent to me. I won't judge. I mean, like, in general. I– yeah."

Mark frowned. "...Thanks, I guess."

The car went silent again.

At around eight, the trio arrived at Riverview.

The moment Mark stepped out of the car, he confirmed Riverview was absolutely nothing like the quiet, suburban town of Salfran Bay.

Despite it being fairly late, the sound of traffic blared through the streets. Twenty-story buildings lined the block, with lights and signs flashing on every single one of them. The sidewalks were crowded with people, and Mark was forced to stand on the curb just to avoid it all.

"Ah, the big city!" Ellie spread her arms, staring up at the sky.

Lincoln stepped out last. "This is actually one of the smaller cities in the country, in terms of both population and area. We're just downtown."

Mark glanced at his phone. "Okay. Alita lives down the block." Mark pointed to his right. "Let's go."

The trio made their way through the street, turning into the apartment building.

The apartment lobby was sparsely furnished– a couch and a coffee table were tucked into one side of the room, and on the other side, there was a counter, with a man behind it scrawling something onto a piece of paper.

Mark, Lincoln, and Ellie began to walk over to the elevator, but the manager looked up at them and gave them a slight wave.

"I'm sorry, I don't recognize you... do you live here?"Mark froze, half-convinced that they were screwed before Ellie spoke up.

"...It's Lisa." Ellie glared at the manager. "We've *met*. I've lived here for a year."

The man immediately turned bright red. "Oh! I'm so sorry!" Looking away, the manager began to 'nervously shuffle through some papers. "G–Go right ahead, uh, Lisa."

The three walked past the counter. As soon as they were out of earshot of the man, Mark grinned at Ellie. "You're *good*."

Ellie smirked, looking satisfied with herself.

Lincoln pressed the elevator button. "She lives in apartment 5-C." He said as the elevator door opened.

The three slid into the elevator, Mark pressing the button for the fifth floor.

After a couple of moments, the door opened with a ding. The three walked out into a beige hallway, stopping at apartment 5-C.

"I– should we just knock?" Mark asked.

"No," Lincoln replied.

"Why?"

"There's a doorbell."

"...Oh."

Rolling her eyes, Ellie rang it.

The three waited for a minute. Just as Mark was beginning to think no one was home, the door opened.

The person that greeted the trio was decidedly not Alita. It was a young girl that couldn't have been older than Mark, at least not by much. She was short and pasty, with an impossibly frizzy head of bright red hair, and a look on her face that made it clear that she was not happy to see any of them.

"What do you want?" She asked, cocking an eyebrow.

"Uh... hi." Ellie started. "Does... Alita Estia live here?"

The girl's face darkened before she slammed the door shut.

Mark stared at the door. "What the hell?" Mark walked up to the doorbell, ringing it multiple times in rapid succession.

The door opened again. "Go away!" The girl shouted with a snarl.

"We do not want any trouble," Lincoln said. "We simply wish to speak with Alita–"

"Oh, fuck off!" The girl shouted. "You guys think it's sooo funny, screwing with the crazy lady!" A pained expression flickered across her face. "Can't... can't you just leave us alone?"

Ellie tilted her head. "Crazy lady...?"

The girl glowered at Ellie. "Don't play dumb. People always come by, asking Alita questions about The People of the Nine, even though they... they're hurting her!"

"I think you misunderstand us," Lincoln replied. "While we do intend to question her about the People of the Nine, it's not for our amusement or our selfish gain."The girl stared at Lincoln, before scoffing. "Do you think I'm dumb?" The girl began to close the door again.

"Azrog!" Mark blurted out. The girl stopped to stare at him, her eyes wide as saucers.

"...Does that word mean anything to you?"

Wordlessly, the girl opened the door, motioning for them to come in.

"...and then we drove over here." Mark finished recounting an abridged version of their tale.

Mark, Ellie, and Lincoln were seated on the couch, the frizzy-haired girl seated on a chair across from them, a coffee table separating them.

"...Okay." She said, letting out a long sigh. "The rumors were right. About the People of the Nine getting all their information from Alita." She clenched her fists in her lap. "I... it broke her heart. Everything the cult did, especially to that poor girl, it... she blamed herself." The girl leaned forward in the chair, rubbing her temples. "She's... she's *sick* now, because of it. She can't even take care of herself. My mom– her sister– used to do it... but... she died, so... it's my job now." The girl glared down at the floor. "And... news reporters, people pulling pranks or *whatever*, they... they keep coming by. They think it's funny to mess with her. That's why I..."

The room was silent for a while. Mark stared at the girl, feeling a pang of sympathy for her.

"Mom told me about everything. All her visions. I never really believed it. But... recently. Alita's... Alita's been... distressed. She keeps saying stuff about Lila Carter, becoming an Azrog. And it *has* been thirty years. If what you're saying is true... maybe..."

"I– kid, what's your name?" Mark asked.

"Rita. *And I'm not a kid.*" She added, with a weak bite.

"Rita... can we talk to her? I get it if we shouldn't, but..." Mark trailed off.

"She can't talk well. But you can try." Rita stood up, motioning them to follow her.

"She's in that room." She pointed to a bedroom down the short hallway.

"I– just... please. Be nice to her."

Rita led the three down the hall. Gently, she creaked open the bedroom door.

"Auntie? You have visitors."

Fully opening the door, Alita was crouching on the foot of her bed. She was clad in a worn, floral dress. Despite Lincoln saying she was in her sixties, she looked nearly twice as old as that– her tousled hair was as white as a sheet, and she was frail enough that she looked like she'd turn to dust in the breeze.

"Lila. Lila is mad. She is sad. She'll hurt people." Alita muttered.

Ellie softly spoke. "Alita... we–"

"She *wants* to be an Azrog." The woman rasped, sounding desperate. "She murdered the brunette with the green eyes!"

Mark froze, remembering Eric's brown hair and mossy eyes.

"Why would she kill people?" Rita asked, a bit pale.

"She *wants* to be an Azrog. She wants to kill this Earth! But her conduit hadn't killed anyone." Alita curled up in the bed, visibly shaking. "So she made her conduit kill people! And now... she'll destroy the world, if she succeeds at three!"

Mark's heart raced as he wrapped his head around everything Alita had said, implicitly and explicitly.

"So... Lila's a demon now." Mark started, turning to the others. "Whoever did the ritual didn't kill anybody beforehand. So, she possessed whoever did it, then *made* them kill people, so she could turn into an Azrog, and just... destroy the world?"

"Fuck..." Ellie said weakly.

After a deafening moment of silence, Lincoln spoke up, turning to Alita.

"...We understand what you are saying. And we have a way to stop Lila. Do not worry."

Alita stared wide-eyed at Lincoln. "Thank you! Thank you!" She yelled, smiling. "Defeat the boy with the blonde hair!"

"Blonde...hair?" Mark asked.

"The conduit– it's him! The muscular boy of your age! The one with the blonde hair, the criminal, the son of the mayor! Stop him!" The woman cried, still grinning maniacally at them.

"It... it was *Axel*?" Ellie shook her head. "I...I knew he wasn't a... but..."

Mark cupped his mouth in his hands, trying to make sense of what had just happened.

"Who the hell is Axel?" Rita hissed.

"He is our schoolmate, the son of the mayor of Salfran Bay, and a notorious sociopath," Lincoln replied. "And if what Alita said was true, the summoner of Lila Carter and the killer of Eric Jacobs."

Mark shook his head. "Wait– how does *Axel* know about this? Any of it?"

Lincoln paused for a bit before he replied. "Do you remember that he goes to the library?"

Their brief confrontation with Axel there flashed through his head.

"Then... he found the book. And... and he..." Mark trailed off.

He turned to Lincoln, fidgeting with his sleeve. "Okay... what do we do? How do we stop them?"

"Well, we have to do so by the end of the... week..." Lincoln trailed off, staring off into space for a long moment.

"No...no no no no," Lincoln whispered hoarsely, shaking his head.

"Lincoln...?" Ellie asked.

"It's been a week since Eric Jacobs died. Lila was possessing Axel when Eric Jacobs died. Lila is almost certainly possessing Axel right now."

Mark's chest dropped. "Fuck. I– we– we gotta go! Now!" Mark frantically tugged at his jacket, Ellie, Lincoln, and Rita following him outside.

Ellie sped outrageously the entire way back, condensing a four-hour trip into two.

But when they drove into Salfran Bay, where sirens were ringing and red and blue lights were flashing all around them, they were too late.

Ellie drove over to Masin Street, where a crowd had gathered, surrounding an ambulance.

Climbing out of the car, they rushed into the scene. "What happened?" Ellie asked a middle-aged man.

The man turned to the four of them, dismay clear on his face. "Nina Cristen hung herself. They just found her."

Mark froze. He had heard that name floating around Salfran Bay before– she owned the Six-Bun Bakery.

Mark had never met her, but he overheard a girl gushing about how she always gave her and her friends free sweets. Whenever she was brought up, everyone seemed to fawn over how kind she was.

And now, she was reduced to a victim.

Mark stared at the now shut-down bakery, at the cartoonish smiles drawn all over the windows.

Feeling nauseous, he ran away from the scene.

"*Fuck.* FUCK!" Mark slumped over on the bench.

Quietly, Lincoln sat down next to him. "Mark. We will–"

"What? We'll *what*? People are *dead!*"

A grin crept up onto Mark's face, and he began to cackle hysterically.

"We... we can't fucking change that! No matter what we do, we can't! Even if we did everything in the *world* we could, Eric and Nina are dead, and they're gonna *stay dead!*"

"Mark, calm down! *Please!*" Gently, Ellie leaned over and rested a hand on his shoulder.

The sickening touch made him tense, but he didn't pull away until the delirium had subsided.

And he was left sitting on the bench, mortified at what he had just done.

"I... that wasn't– I... I'm sorry." Mark stammered.

"It– it's fine," Ellie replied, quietly.

The air was stagnant for a while before Lincoln spoke. "No more murders have happened. Lila is likely no longer possessing Axel. We have to figure out how to stop Lila from committing her next murder. Rita," He addressed her, despite not looking at her, "You likely know more about demons than the rest of us. Do you have any ideas?"

"...You could kill Axel."

The three went completely still at that.

"...*what?*" Mark whispered, slowly turning to Rita.

Rita looked down. "...If Axel summoned Lila then... if we killed him, she couldn't get to anyone else, right?"

"I– no. No." Ellie frantically shook her head. "Axel's a *jackass*, I'm not saying he isn't, but... we can't *kill him!*"

Rita glared at Ellie. "Hey, he *summoned* Lila, even though he *knew* she could get us all killed! Look, even if I don't know Axel, I can tell he's got this coming!"

"Wait a minute." Lincoln interrupted the two of them. "A question just occurred to me, and I'd like to share the question."

Rita glared. "Dude, what–"Ellie cut her off with a sharp glance.

"Why does Axel only kill when he is possessed?" Lincoln asked.

Mark frowned. "What–?"

"Rather than kill three people before commencing the ritual, even though that would be the simpler option, he commenced the ritual, and only kills when Lila is possessing him." Lincoln tilted his head down. "Why is that?"

After no one said anything for a while, Lincoln spoke again.

"It's possible he doesn't know he is being possessed."

Rita stared at Lincoln in disbelief. "Wait– that– *that doesn't make any sense!* If– he didn't *know* he was gonna get possessed, then... there's no way he knew how to summon her!"

"That's not true," Lincoln replied. "The possession, and its conditions, were only mentioned in a footnote. It's possible that he didn't read it."

"Wait, wait." Mark shook his head. "If... if he was *seriously* gonna summon a demon, then... wouldn't he look that whole book inside out?"

"He would," Lincoln said, bluntly. "Except he might not have been going to *seriously* summon a demon. Like Bloody Mary."

Mark took a moment to piece together what he was saying. "I... you mean... he didn't think it'd actually work?"

Lincoln nodded as Ellie turned to him, confused. "I- but *why*? Why would he do it, if he didn't think it'd work?"

"Like... have you ever played Bloody Mary before?" Mark asked, echoing what Lincoln had said. When Ellie hesitantly nodded, he continued. "You... you *knew* it wouldn't work, but you still did it, right? Maybe... maybe it was like that?"

Ellie gaped at him. "I..."

Rita grimaced. "Okay... *if* that's true- pretty big *if*, but whatever- we... we can't kill this guy."

Ellie nodded.

"I don't like Axel anymore than you guys do," she said, nodding at Lincoln and Mark.

"But... if he didn't know what he was doing... he...he doesn't deserve to *die*."

"I... you're right." Mark nodded.

"You're right." Lincoln echoed. "But that may not be the answer to my earlier question. If needed, we should confront Axel. Also, now I have another question- why did Lila make Axel only kill one person a week?"

The group went silent again.

"I can't answer my question," Lincoln said. "If necessary, I will later attempt to gather more information, so I can answer my question."

"You talk weird, you know that?" Rita cocked an eyebrow. "Like a stoned college professor."

"Drug stoned or rock stoned?"

"*Moving on*," Mark cut them off, "Rita. Do you have any idea how we can stop Lila *without* killing Axel?"

Rita shook her head. "I can't think of anything. But..."

Rita rifled through her pockets, pulling out a small, but relatively thick notebook.

"I grabbed this on my way out. These are all my notes on everything Alita's told me."She held it out to Mark, who hesitantly took it.

"Maybe... there's something here. You know where to find me if... if you need me." Rita turned away from them.

"You're not staying?" Ellie asked.

Rita pursed her lips. "I can't... gotta look after Alita. I'll... I'll catch a bus or something." With that, she walked away, leaving Ellie, Mark, and Lincoln to stare at the notebook.

They'd torn the notes out of the book and split them into three sections, with each of them taking one home to read.

He'd told the others he'd flip through his section the moment he got home, but Mark couldn't even look at the notes without feeling sick.

He'd look at them tomorrow morning. Or he'd guilt-trip Ellie into doing it for him.

God, Mark hated himself for thinking that.

Hiding the notes behind a lamp so that they were out of his line of sight, he pulled his sketchbook out.

He stared at a blank page for about ten minutes, before putting it away and curling up into bed.

He didn't sleep that night.

"...Did you find anything?" Ellie asked.

Mark shook his head. He'd forced himself to read the notes that morning but had come up empty-handed. All he found were more horrific rituals completely irrelevant to the situation.

"Me either. Let's just hope Lincoln found something."

That morning was torture. Everywhere he turned, someone was talking about Nina or Eric, and he'd have to restrain himself from starting a fight or running out of the room. Mark knew he was being pathetic, but he wasn't asking for much when he said he wanted to forget everything for a moment, was he?

Mark felt his arms shaking at his sides when he entered the cafeteria. The hundreds of overlapping conversations rang through his ears, and he was half-tempted to crawl under a table.

"Mark. Are you okay?" Mark flinched when he felt a hand on his shoulder, but relaxed when he realized that it was Lincoln.

"Y-yeah. I'm fine." Mark said, trying to ignore the crushing feeling in his chest.

"Sit down. With Ellie and me." Mark felt himself nod, as he was guided by Lincoln to their usual table. This time, Ellie sat there as well.

"Hey, you two." Ellie frowned at Mark. "Is everything okay? You look kinda..."

"Everything's fine." Mark swallowed, trying to moisten his throat. "Yeah."

Lincoln nodded. "I found something in my section of the notes." Lincoln took out a single page, showing it to Ellie and Mark.

'If a human is possessed by a demon, it can be exorcized if the human drinks enough holy water—usually an obscene amount. How much may depend

on the demon, but one will likely never be forced to drink beyond three or four gallons.'

Mark blinked. "Do you think...?"

"Yes. Even if I didn't, it's our only option."

"I..." Mark reviewed the note in his head, feeling a bit giddy.

For the first time in a while, there was an actual, straightforward solution available to their problems. Sure, Mark didn't know where they were going to get holy water, or how they would get Axel to drink it, but their answer was there. They wouldn't have to go on another goose chase.

They could stop Lila. They could stop people from dying.

"This... this could work!" Mark grinned. "I... we can... this–"

"Yeah," Ellie said, looking breathless as well. "We can *do this*."

"I agree." Lincoln shot the two a rare smile. "However, we still have to come up with a plan."

Lincoln paused for a bit before he replied. "How would you two like to come to my house after school today?"

Ellie frowned. "Shit. I promised Kelsey I'd come over after school. Uh... text me if you need me, but... yeah. Sorry."

Lincoln turned to Mark. "How about you?" Mark stared at Lincoln, his grin widening.

"That'd be great."

Lincoln's house was a little thing near the center of town. Mark walked over through the front yard, with a bit of a bounce in his step.

Ringing the doorbell, an older woman in a yellow sundress greeted him.

"Hi... is Lincoln home?"

The woman clapped her hands together, grinning. "Ooh! You must be that nice boy Lincoln was telling us about! Come in!"

Hesitantly, Mark followed the lady in, wondering how skewed Lincoln's perception of him was. *Nice boy?*

"Uh... you're Ms. Gray, right? I–"

The woman cut him off with a shake of her head. "Oh, please, that's my mother's name! I'm Lincoln's mother, Marleene. This is my husband, Vernon!" She gestured at a man with graying who had walked up to the two. "Vernon, this is Lincoln's friend!"

"Oh?" Vernon let out a hearty laugh. "You know, son, we've been dying to meet you. Lincoln's told us so much about you– only good stuff, I promise!"

"Oh, uh... really?" Mark asked, vaguely aware of the warmth creeping up into his face.Marleene beamed. "We're so glad Lincoln has a good friend." The chipper woman's face darkened. "You know, he was very unpopu–"

"Hello, Mark, mom, dad." A voice cut Marleene off. Lincoln walked up to them, gripping Mark by the shoulder. "Come to my room, Mark."

Mark followed Lincoln, who was still firmly gripping him, through the halls, eventually stopping at a beige door, which Lincoln cracked open.

It looked like a typical seventeen-year-old's bedroom, if unrealistically tidy. There was a bookshelf, a desk, and a couple of lamps all tucked against the back wall, a simple linen green rug spread out on the floor. There was only one thing in the room that truly stood out to Mark.

"A... racecar bed?" Mark blinked.

Lincoln sat on the foot of the flashy red bed with a sigh. "Like I said before, my parents seem to think- not literally- that I am ten years younger than I actually am."

With a slight chuckle, Mark sat next to him. "This... aside," Mark vaguely gestured at the bed, "Your parents seem pretty cool."

Lincoln pursed his lips, not looking at him. "Are you being sarcastic?" Lincoln tilted his head.

"I'm bad at sarcasm."

"What- no." Mark frowned. "They were... nice, I guess. Why would I be-"

"You weren't." Lincoln looked down. "I'm sorry. I was wrong."

"I–it's fine." Mark shook his head. "But, why would that be–" Mark cut himself off when he heard a knock at the door. Marleene pushed it open, walking inside.

"Hi, Linky!" Marleene trilled, holding a plate and a pitcher. "I made cookies and punch! Don't fight over them!" She placed them both on Lincoln's bedside table.

"So, Mark, what grade are you in?" Marleene, uninvited, sat next to Mark, close enough that their thighs were touching. He tried to scoot away as subtly as possible.

"Uh... eleventh. Like Lincoln." He nodded at the curly-haired boy.

"Oh, a junior!" Marleene shot a wide grin at him that vaguely reminded Mark of a feral animal. "What colleges are you thinking about?"

"Uh... I haven't thought about it yet." Mark lied, knowing he didn't have the grades, the money, or the aspirations for college.

"Ah. Well, Lincoln here is thinking about Harvard! Isn't that something?" Marleene reached across Mark to pinch an unreactive Lincoln's cheek.

"I'm slated to become valedictorian, I have a 5.0 GPA, and I'll likely get a perfect score on the SAT."

While Mark gawked at Lincoln, Marleene giggled. "Right! Keep trying!" Standing up, she walked around to Lincoln, planting a kiss on his forehead. "I'll leave you two be for a bit. If you need anything, call me! Love you, cookie!" With a parting smile, she walked out of the room, leaving the door open.

With a sigh, Lincoln got up and closed the door.

"She's... touchy," Mark said, rubbing the side of his thigh.

"Yes." Lincoln sat back down next to Mark. "Do you like chocolate chips?" Lincoln asked, looking over at the plate of cookies.

"No, I'm the one guy in the world that doesn't like chocolate– *yes*, I like chocolate chip."

When Lincoln looked visibly confused, Mark continued. "That– that first part was sarcasm."

"Ah." Standing up, Lincoln brought the cookies over to the foot of the bed.

Sliding one off of the plate, Mark took a big bite out of a cookie.

"Whoa. These are pretty good." Mark said, his voice a bit muffled.

"For all of her flaws, my mother is an excellent baker," Lincoln said, taking a cookie for himself.

Swallowing the cookie, Mark turned to Lincoln. "Is... is she always like that?"

"Not always– just most of the time," Lincoln replied, taking a bite.

"I... oh. How...?" Mark asked, trailing off.

"Mom is a good mom. She means well." Lincoln replied, cutting him off. "But I wish she treated me more like an adult. I want to grow up."

Mark hummed in sympathy. "Have you... tried talking to her?"

"Yes, but she never takes me too seriously." Lincoln stared at the ground.

"I... that sucks."

After a brief lull of silence, Mark spoke again. "So... the plan?"

"Let's come up with one," Lincoln replied, lowering his voice.

The plan they came up with was undeniably risky but feasible.

There was no chance that Axel would go with them willingly. So, on the day Lila was supposed to possess him, they would get Axel alone, and drug him. Lincoln had insisted on this, saying that, concerningly enough, he knew how to make chloroform. Reluctantly, Mark agreed.

Then, they would throw him into Ellie's basement. After texting her, she confirmed that she had a basement that they could access without running into her parents.

They'd take Axel out, tie him up, and, once Lila possessed him, they would force them to drink holy water until Lila was gone.

"Okay. But where can we get holy water?" Mark asked, leaning forward as he cupped his mouth in his hands.

"It's available on Amazon," Lincoln replied.

"I– really?" Mark asked, his eyes wide.

"I was surprised, too," Lincoln said. "Now–" Mark's phone buzzed. He waved a little at Lincoln, before pulling it out to check it.

Rick: *Come home. Your therapy sessions in an hour.*

With a sigh, Mark tucked his phone back into his pocket, standing up. "That was Rick. He wants me home."

"What for? It's not too late."

"...He thinks I need therapy," Mark muttered, after a brief pause. "Which– which I don't, obviously. I– I'm fine." Running his hand through his hair, Mark chuckled a little. "I'm just gonna go in, pretend to listen, then leave. I–"

"I don't recommend that." Lincoln said, cutting him off.

Mark stared at him, cocking his head. "What... what do you mean?"

Lincoln stood up from the bed so that he was level with Mark. "Therapy could be good for you." he replied. "Even mentally well people can benefit from it. It–"

"Well, yeah." Mark snorted. "But, let's be real, I don't– I– it's a waste of time. I mean, it's not like I'm *crazy*, don't you get..." At that last word, Lincoln went completely still. Mark trailed off.

"I– did I say something I shouldn't have?" He said, a bit nervously.

"'Craziness' and therapy do not overlap," Lincoln said.

"I– uh–"

"Tell me, Mark– am I crazy, then?" Lincoln tilted his head, somehow making the action look menacing.

"...*What?*"

"You heard what I said. I've attended therapy before. Does that make me crazy?" For the first time since Mark met him, Lincoln looked genuinely angry.

"I– no, I–"

"I was diagnosed with Autism Spectrum Disorder when I was ten. It caused problems for me in my everyday life. I was sent to a therapist that helped me learn strategies to be more comfortable with myself. With others. I still have problems, but I can manage them."

Lincoln grinned, but for once, Mark hated how it looked on his face. "But of course, the fact that I needed help makes me sick. Because therapy is for crazy people."

"Wait, wait... *you*–?" Mark stared at Lincoln, before frantically shaking his head. "I– that wasn't– Lincoln, I'm so *sorry*. I didn't mean..." He felt his face burn with guilt and shame.

"That's how it sounded to me." Lincoln glared at the ground.

Mark opened his mouth to say something, but Lincoln spoke before he could. "Please, give me a moment."

Closing his mouth with an audible click, he watched the anger gradually fade from Lincoln's face.

"Alright. I'll speak now." Lincoln finally said. "You made me angry. I don't like it when people say I'm crazy or weird. Especially not my friends– though, I haven't had any in a long time. I've been called that in the past, in much worse contexts than this. But I know it wasn't your intention to offend me."

"Lincoln, I'm really sorry." Mark shook his head. "I didn't know you actually went to... to therapy. And I didn't know you had... you know."

"Again, I know it wasn't your intention. So, I forgive you." Lincoln glanced off to the side. "But I wish you wouldn't conflate mental illness with insanity."

"I– I *don't*." Mark sat back on the bed. "I... I know, it was fucked up to say that. And I'm not trying to say it *wasn't*. It's just..." Mark wrung his hands together in his lap, staring down at them.

"I– when I was a kid. I... my foster parents kept saying that I was crazy. For attention, or so they wouldn't have to deal with me, or *whatever*." Mark laughed bitterly. "They kept sending me to these quacks, and they'd... they'd drug me up, or tell me I was a psycho." Mark wrapped his arms around his ribs, feeling pathetic. "I... I *hated it*. I always... felt so..." Mark let out a heavy sigh. "And the worst part was that... sometimes, I... I honestly didn't know if they were right or not. I kept wondering if they were all telling the truth. Maybe I *was* a psychopath. Or... or..." His voice cracked. "And I *know* that they're wrong. But... whenever I fuck something up or... whatever, I... there's this voice in the back of my head that says that... they were right."

Mark squeezed his forehead in his head, leaning backward so that his back hit the mattress, his lower legs still dangling off the side of the bed. "I... I don't ever want to feel like that again. And... I feel like I do if I go to therapy. A-and even if it doesn't... it'll still remind me of..." Mark trailed off.

"...I'm sorry, this wasn't- I shouldn't have-"

"Mark, stand up."

"...what?" Sitting up on the bed, he stared at Lincoln, who was meeting his eyes.

"Stand up." Hesitantly, Mark did what he said.

Then, Lincoln gently, but firmly, pulled him into a hug.

Stunned, Mark stood still as Lincoln pulled him close for a few moments, before backing away.

"Should I not have done that?" Lincoln asked, looking uncertain.

"I..." Mark stared at Lincoln, before shaking his head. "That... I'm not big on touching."

When Lincoln looked guilty, Mark quickly added, "But I get what you were trying to do. And... I think it worked. Thanks."

Lincoln looked down. "I'm glad it worked."

"...Just... ask next time, okay?" Mark scratched at the back of his neck. "It... like I said, I- I usually don't like people touching me. But... it isn't really *bad* if... if it's you."

"...Oh," Lincoln replied, quieter than normal.

Feeling that he hadn't said that right, Mark felt the urge to elaborate.

"C-cause we're... *friends*, so it... it's fine." He found that his throat had tightened, and he had to force the words out.

"I understand." Lincoln nodded, not looking at Mark. "And I'm glad that you feel comfortable with me."

The room was silent for an agonizing moment before Lincoln spoke up again. "You should go to your therapy session now. But I ask you to please, talk and listen to them. It could be beneficial, considering everything that's happened in the past week."

Mark felt a twisting sensation in his stomach at the mention of therapy. "I... I get what you're saying, but... I... I don't know if I can do it. *Talk*. Especially to... to a–"

Lincoln cut him off. "From what you've told me about Rick, I don't think he would send you to someone incompetent." Lincoln's eyes met Mark's. "You have had bad experiences in the past. You have the right to be wary. But you should know that you can probably trust this person."

Nervously, Mark bit the inside of his cheek. "I– I *know that*... but... I still– I– I'm *scared*."

"You can do it," Lincoln replied, in a gentle voice. "You're a brave person. You'll manage it."

Mark stared at Lincoln. He wanted to remind him that he wasn't brave, not in the slightest.

But he also wanted to believe in him. He wanted what he said to be true.

So, hesitantly, Mark nodded at him. "Okay. I'll try."

When Lincoln smiled at him, he muttered something he couldn't remember and left the house.

"Hello, Mark. I'm Dr. Lichen."

Mark, uncomfortably, shifted in his seat. "...hey."

The woman– short and skinny, with a bob cut– put her elbows on the table between them, tenting her fingers together. "

So... how have you been feeling, recently?"

"Honestly? Kinda like, uh... well... shit." Mark said, as eloquently as he could.

"...I see." The woman glanced down, before looking back up at Mark. "Could you elaborate? Why do you feel that way?"

"I... I can't tell you the whole story." Mark looked away, remembering the downright illegal situations he had gotten himself into. Not to mention, he doubted Dr. Lichen would believe him even if he did tell her that there was a homicidal demon haunting the town.

"Everything you say is confidential. You–"

"I know, but... I still can't– I..." Mark trailed off.

"Of course, if you really don't want to share some things, that's alright." The woman gave Mark a small smile. "But feel free to share whatever you're comfortable with."

"I... okay. So... when I moved here... I found a dead body. I think you heard about that." The therapist nodded.

"And... it fucked– sorry, messed with my head. I–"

"If you want to curse, it's fine. I don't judge." Dr. Lichen gave Mark a cheeky wink. "Sorry, go on?"

Chuckling a little, Mark continued. "I... I kept seeing it. In my head. And all the kids at school thought I was crazy, cause... you know." Mark covered his mouth with his hands, letting out a heavy sigh.

"I... for a moment, I thought I *was* crazy. But... my friend helped pull me out of it. But... I still, sometimes, think that I..." Mark went quiet, and stared down at the table.

"Mark. You're not crazy." Dr. Lichen replied, after a brief silence. "You were in a situation that would've been scary for almost anyone. It's only natural you'd see things. Besides, your reaction didn't hurt anyone, did it?"

"...No. I guess not... but..." Mark stared down at the desk. "I... I still feel really stupid. And crazy. Not even just about what happened. It... it wasn't even... just. I... I don't like it when people say I'm... crazy, or whatever. It... I..."

"Well, no one would want to be labeled like that." Dr. Lichen hummed. "But it seems like it affects you especially."

"...Yeah. I guess." Mark nervously fiddled with his hair. "I... when I was a kid... I–"

Mark's throat suddenly seized up with fear.

He couldn't tell her about anything that they did. Not today.

"... never mind."

Dr. Lichen pursed her lips, looking unconvinced, before moving on to talk about something else.

Mark left Dr. Lichen's office that day feeling a little lighter than when he came, but not by much.

Avoiding mention of demons or cults, he had talked about all the feelings he had over the past week. Dr. Lichen nodded along, giving her own opinion on some things, but never shoving them down his throat.

Mark thought that someday, he might be able to trust her.

"How'd it go?" Rick asked, holding the steering wheel.

"Honestly... it went okay." Mark leaned back in the car seat, staring out the passenger window.

"...can I go again next week?"

Rick stopped, looking a bit surprised, before nodding.

"Yeah. I'll set it up."

"Thanks." Mark glanced back at him, to find that Rick was smiling.

When they got home, Mark opened his sketchbook, and, for the first time in a while, he found himself itching to draw.

He drew a single tulip, sprouting from the ground. It was a simple sketch, compared to his other drawings, but Mark found that he loved it. He put away his sketchbook, and had just laid back in bed when his phone buzzed.

Lincoln: *How did the therapy session go?*

Mark: *better than the last guy.*

Mark: *didnt even talk to me. just wrote me up for thorazine and called it a day.*

Lincoln: *:/*

Mark: *seriously, it went okay.*

Mark: *its nice to have someone to talk to*

Lincoln: *Am I chopped liver?*

Lincoln: *I am joking. I am kidding.*

Mark: *i got that.*

Mark: *and you know what i meant*

Lincoln: *That it's nice to have someone to talk to who is a professional?*

Lincoln: *If it's that, I understood.*

Mark: *...yeah*

Mark: *if you don't mind, how's therapy for you?*

Lincoln: *I don't mind. I'll answer.*

Lincoln: *I talk about my life and my feelings, and my therapist gives advice about both of them.*

Lincoln: *But, it is hard to go sometimes.*

Lincoln: *Sometimes I don't want to tell them anything. Sometimes I think I can deal with things on my own.*

Lincoln: *It's hard, but I still go because it's mostly good for me.*

Mark: *huh*

Mark: *good to know, ig*

Neither of them wrote anything for a few minutes. Mark stared at his phone the entire time.

Mark: *what are you doing now*

Lincoln: *I'm texting you.*

Mark: *fuck you (kidding)*

Mark: *what else?*

Lincoln: *I'm finishing off the cookies and punch from earlier.*

Lincoln then sent a picture of a half-empty glass of punch, next to a plate that held a cookie with a large bite taken out of it, all laid out on his nightstand.

Mark: *cool*

Lincoln: *What are you doing?*

Mark: *nothing.*

Lincoln: *That's not true. You're texting me.*

Mark: *fine. other than that, nothing.*

Lincoln: *I'm assuming you're breathing.*

Mark: *i'm a ghost*

Lincoln: Oh. 0_0

Mark: *wait*

Mark: DID YOU JUST ASSUME MY SPECIES

Lincoln: *I did, and I'm sorry. I'll take this as a lesson, and I'll work on myself in the future.*

Mark: *boo ghostphobe*

Mark laughed to himself but paused to read over his past few texts, and cringed a little.

Mark: *...i feel like im acting weird*

Mark: *tell me if i am and ill stop.*

Lincoln: *You're not.*

Mark: *k. good.*

Mark: *its just that your easier to talk to then everyone else*

Mark: *and were not talking in person*

Mark: *so im not that scared of saying something dumb.*

Lincoln: *I like you when you're not that scared of saying something dumb.*

Lincoln: *It's like I'm talking more to the real you.*

Mark: *real me? am i a robot somehow*

Lincoln: *I'm not sure, but I don't think so.*

Lincoln: *But when I say the 'real you', I think you know what I mean.*

Mark: *i do. kidding again.*

Lincoln: *Anyway, I like the real you.*

At that, Mark paused, feeling himself going a bit warm.

Mark: *what do you like about 'the real me'*

Lincoln didn't respond for a long moment. Right when Mark was beginning to type out an apology, he replied.

Lincoln: *The real you is nice, funny, and brave. They treated me like a normal person. Most people don't do that.*

Lincoln: *They are empathetic and honest. They are passionate.*

Lincoln: *They are my friend.*

Mark gaped at his phone. Wiping a sweaty, clammy hand off on his jeans, he typed out a reply.

Mark: *ngl they sound pretty awesome*

Lincoln: *You are.*

At that, he hastily excused himself from the conversation before collapsing back into his bed.

His face was hot. Feverishly so. And his heart was definitely beating faster than normal.

But somehow, the sensations weren't unwelcome.

Still feeling warm, Mark curled up in the bed, tossing a pillow over his head, and tried to will himself to sleep.

Mark had been completely tuning his world history teacher out when his phone buzzed in his pocket.

Strategically slipping it onto his lap, which was obscured by the desk, he fixed himself so that he could see the phone, but his teacher couldn't.

Tapping the notification, he saw that it was from Ellie.

Ellie: *U busy after school?*

Mark: *im in class right now*

Ellie: *So am I!*

Mark: *why*

Ellie: *wanna hang out?*

Mark frowned at his phone.

The two had made it clear between them that, while they were on decent terms, they weren't friends.

And yet, Ellie had just invited him to hang out as if they were.

Out of a mixture of impulsivity and curiosity, Mark typed out his reply.

Mark: *okay, i guess? where?*

Ellie: *ida's ice cream!*

Mark had begun to type again when he heard someone loudly clear their throat.

He looked up to face his history teacher, glaring down at him.

He gulped.

It turned out that, for a man who assigned several hours of homework a night, Mr. Richards was pretty reasonable.

He had taken his phone away for the day but had given it back after school, without even writing him up or calling Rick.

Now, he was using the same phone to navigate to Ida's Ice Cream, a store he found was only a block or two away from the diner where they had previously gathered.

The door chimed when he opened it, and he was greeted by Ellie, sitting at a small table, cheerfully waving him over.

"Hey." He said, sitting across from Ellie.

"Hi, Mark!" Ellie glanced behind him. "What flavor do you want?" Looking back, he glanced at the menu displayed on the wall behind the counter.

Mark felt his mouth fall open a bit as he realized something that he should have realized a while ago.

"Uh... I don't have any cash." He had been so fixated on Ellie's request that he failed to think about its finer implications- like how she had invited him to a place where one was expected to spend money.

Ellie waved her hand dismissively. "It's fine! On me."

"Oh. O–Okay?"

Ellie motioned for him to walk up to the counter with her. He ordered a cheap milkshake, while Ellie got a sundae.

"So... uh–" Mark said after they sat back down. "Why... why'd you invite me out today?"

Ellie looked taken aback at that, before she stared down at her sundae, looking contemplative.

"I..." She picked her ice cream with a plastic spoon. "I– was this a bad idea?" She asked, more to herself than Mark.

"It's just– we've done a lot, together, and... and, I know what you said, about us being friends, but... I wanted to get to know you." Ellie picked the cherry off the top of her sundae, twirling the stem between her fingers.

"M–maybe this was a bad idea. If you want, you can go." Ellie gestured at the door, still not looking up."

Mark stared at Ellie, before glancing off to the side, pursing his lips.

"You... you paid." Mark started. "For the shake. I... I guess we can talk for a little."

Ellie visibly perked up. "Oh... uh, cool!" She grinned, looking a bit sheepish. "So... what'd you think about that math test?"

Mark snorted. "I don't *want* to think about it. No way I didn't fail hard."

Ellie gawked, pointing at herself. "S-same! All my friends said that it was so *easy,* a-and I was like, *what are you talking about?*"

Mark leaned back in his chair, glaring up at the ceiling. "You have any idea what the hell a derivative is?"

Ellie threw her hands up in the air. "*Not a clue!*"

Mark shook his head. "I swear, half the time, Ms. Bite's making shit up."

"Yeah! Either Calculus is bullshit, or she's friggin' insane!"

"Could be both."The two stared at each other for a moment, before laughing in unison.

"...and then, the entire set came crashing down!" Ellie slammed her hands on the table to emphasize her words. "Whole play was ruined!"

"Why'd they even need that many extras?" Mark asked, bemused.

"You tell me!"

Mark laughed, before glancing at his phone. "It's six already?" Mark sprung up from the table. "Shit. Gotta go. Uh... I'll see you–"

"Wait!" Ellie stood with him. "I don't think I live that far from you. I...I can walk with you! If... if you want."

Mark stared at Ellie for a moment, before starting toward the door.

"Sure." He turned his head to smile at her. "Come on."Ellie practically bounced outside.

The two walked in silence for a couple of blocks, before Ellie finally spoke.

"Hey, Mark?" She asked, glancing at him.

"...yeah?"

"Uh... there's something I wanna ask you."

"...okay...?"

"So... uh..." Ellie fidgeted a bit, while still walking. "I remember what you said. That... that you didn't wanna be friends. And I *get that*. I do. But... I... I wanted to know if that was still true."

At that, Mark stopped walking. Ellie kept moving forward, before realizing that he wasn't following, and paused as well, turning around to face him.

"You... you wanna be friends?" Mark asked, dumbly.

"I..." Ellie fiddled with a piece of her hair. "I mean, we've been through a lot, and... yeah. I guess." Ellie stared down at the ground. "I- It's fine if you still don't, but- do you?"

Mark stared dumbly at Ellie for a long moment.

He remembered how Ellie had stood up for him. How much she had helped him and Lincoln throughout the case. How she had shown him sympathy and had been willing to let him vent his thoughts and feelings to her.

He was willing to befriend Lincoln. So why not Ellie?

"...Okay. Yeah. I... I think we can." Mark said, nervously scratching at the back of his neck.

"I... really?" Ellie asked, a grin creeping up on her face. "G-Great! That's... yeah!"

Bashfully, Mark smiled at her.

He was about to say something when a voice cut him off.

"*Ellie?*" A familiar voice trilled.

Mark turned around, to face the blonde girl from the other day strutting up to them, this time with a small posse of girls trailing behind her.

"Oh. Uh... hey, Ashley." Ellie fidgeted with her hands, looking down at the ground. "Uh... what-?"

"Why are you talking with this *creep* again?" Ashley sneered. "Do you *wanna* get murdered?"

The girls behind her laughed like she had just told the funniest joke in the world.

"I– come on. He's cool." Ellie glanced at Mark, looking pained. It happened quickly, but Mark could see her mouth the word 'sorry'.

Ashley scoffed. "He *lied. To the cops!*" She looked down at Ellie, willing her eyes to widen like a puppy's. "Ell, I'm just trying to look out for you. He's *insane*. Everyone knows that."

"He's *not*. He–"

"You know, he's in foster care, right?" Ashley cut her off. Mark couldn't name the look on her face, but whatever it was, he hated it.

"Wh– so what?" Ellie stepped back, looking defensive.

"I mean, *come on*. He's probably there for a reason." Ashley's grin darkened. "You think of that? Maybe, he was so fucked up, his parents *hated him*. So they gave them up. Or–"

Ashley kept talking, but Mark had spaced out as the first decade of his life played out in his mind in a single moment.

His parents swaddling him into bed as they sang him a lullaby. His dad playing a corny parlor game with him. His mom baking, while he begged to help.

A solemn looking cop showing up at his doorstep, telling him that they weren't coming home.

Being shoved into a series of courtrooms, before being taken home by a terrifyingly large man.

Being locked in a tiny cellar for some unknown slight.

Mark stared at Ashley, who began to cackle for some unknown reason.

Rage swarmed within him, and he was prepared to make her regret every word that left her mouth at that moment, but he was stopped by a firm hand tightly gripping his shoulder.

He turned to face Ellie, glaring at Ashley viciously.

Seeing that look on her face quickly soothed his anger, if only a bit.

"What– *what is wrong with you!?*" Ellie snarled. "You... you can't *say* stuff like that!" The girls all looked taken aback, but Ashley quickly recovered, rolling her eyes.

"Please. I–"

"No. No. That wasn't okay." Ellie let go of Mark and began to advance towards Ashley. "You don't know *anything* about him. *You* don't get to say stuff like that."

Ashley glared at Ellie. "Ellie. Come on. This loser? You're overreacting–"

"No. I gotta say this– you're *horrible*. Yeah. I said it. You're just some washed-up *bitch* that thinks that she can pick on others because her dad's rich. And... and I don't know why I put up with you! I– we're not *friends*! And I feel stupid for not saying any of this sooner. I..."

Ashley and her crew all had their jaws, satisfyingly, wide open for a long moment.

Then, Ashley went bright red. "You... you *slut*! I–" Looking lost for words, she turned back to her friends. "Come on, girls. These *freaks* aren't worth our time."

Still looking stunned, the girls walked away, leaving Ellie and Mark standing there in silence.

Neither of them moved for a few minutes until Ellie finally spoke.

"*Oh my god.*" Ellie groaned, crouching down on the ground. "I... I just did that."

Staring at her, Mark awkwardly bent down next to her, not sure of what to say.

"...I- can we talk?"

Mark paused for a moment before he nodded. "...Okay."

"Seriously, kid?" Rick pinched the bridge of his nose, obviously irritated.

"It'll only take a few minutes," Mark said, rubbing the back of his neck as he glanced at Ellie, who stood beside him, awkwardly fidgeting.

Rick let out a long sigh. "...Ten minutes. You get ten minutes, then you have to go home. Got it?"When Ellie nodded, Mark motioned for her to follow him to his room.

"So... you're gonna tell me about...uh..." He gestured vaguely.

"Y-yeah." Ellie sat on the foot of his bed.

"...So... That was Ashley, yeah." She started, absently picking at a loose string on his blanket. "And... I never really liked her. But I- I always put up with her, because all my friends liked her, she was popular, I- you know."

Mark nodded, taking a seat next to her.

"And... it wasn't just Ashley. I- I always wanted to- I tried to make friends with everyone." Ellie chuckled a bit, glancing up at the ceiling. "It... it's nice, to have a lot of people around. You... do you get that?"

"I... I guess." Mark played with the fabric of his jeans. "I mean... I don't... I'm not good. With people. You- you know that." He sighed a bit. "But... yeah. I think I'd get why you'd want that."

"Y-yeah." Ellie hunched forward, adjusting herself, kicking her leg a bit as she did so. "But... I ended up hanging around with people like Ashley. Or Veronica. Or Lisa. And... and I tried to tell myself that they're just joking around, or I'm overreacting, but..." She let out a breath that sounded partway between a sigh and a sob. "They... they can be so *mean*. Even to *me*. I... I kept trying to... to *change* them, or put up with them, or whatever, but then..." Ellie glanced at Mark. "Y-yeah. All... all this happened. And I... on top of all of this, I... I really couldn't take them anymore. And then... Ashley said... *that*, and I... I just kinda snapped. You know?"

Mark shifted a little on the bed. "I... it's good. That you got away from her."

Ellie laughed bitterly. "Seriously? Half the school's gonna think I'm a psycho by tomorrow."

"Yeah, cause I have *no* idea what that's like." Mark scoffed.

"Wait, *no*." Ellie cringed. "I'm sorry, I forgot you were being... I mean, I didn't *forget*, but uh... yeah. Sorry."

"I... it's fine." Mark shook his head. "I get what you mean. And, you're kinda right. It'll suck."Ellie opened her mouth a bit, then closed it, looking away from Mark.

He cleared his throat. "I mean. No one likes me. I don't think Lincoln's gonna be popular anytime soon. And you..." Mark cracked a crooked grin. "Maybe we could do some kind of *Breakfast Club* thing."Ellie turned to Mark, giggling. "We're already kinda ripping off *It*, aren't we?"

"Shit, you're right."

Ellie let out a content breath. "I... thanks. For being cool." She finally said.

Mark scratched at the back of his neck. "Y–yeah."

Ellie opened her mouth to say something before Rick shouted from down the hall.

With a nod, Ellie smiled at him and left.

"...What are we gonna do about him?"

Lincoln glanced up from his book. "Who is 'him'?"

"I... the mayor." Mark leaned against the headboard of his bed.

Lincoln stared at him, before closing his book, and setting it down on the ground, just beside where he sat, curled up in the corner of the bedroom, despite Mark insisting he could sit anywhere else.

"I don't understand. You said you wanted us to 'hang out' without talking about the demon or the mayor or the murders. But you're talking about the mayor. But you said–"

"I–I know. I'm sorry, I just..."

School was off that day, and late that morning, Mark had asked Lincoln to come to Rick's house. A comfortable quiet had settled between the two. Lincoln would occasionally say something, about his book, school, or home, and Mark would reply, and that was it.

Mark enjoyed Lincoln's minimal presence. It soothed him, to have a friend with him, in a context that didn't expect him to say or do much other than sit nearby.

But total peace was unachievable, with the events of the past week constantly fluttering through his head.

Mark didn't bring up Lila herself– she'd be dealt with soon enough. But he had to talk about the mayor.

"I know what I said. But... I know, we got our plan, but what are we gonna do about him?"

Lincoln hugged his knees against his chest, staring down at the ground.

"I don't know. Our priorities shifted from catching the murderer to stopping them. So I don't know."

"Right." Mark let out a long sigh, wrapping his arms behind his neck as he relaxed against the bed.

Lincoln spoke again after a moment. "But I don't want him to get away with what he did, either. When we have gotten rid of Lila, we have to figure out what we should do to ruin him."

"I... how about Arnie? And Grace?" Mark recalled the sight of Lincoln holding the cowardly man at gunpoint, and repressed a shiver. "Maybe we can get them to talk."

"We can't. The mayor is paying them. Probably a lot. They won't talk. We can't."

"I– maybe we can threaten Arnie again, or..." Mark trailed off.

"Arnie would have upped his security, or set up affairs. That would only end badly for us."

"Well, what's your plan, genius?" Mark glared at Lincoln, before screwing his eyes shut. "Sorry."

"I forgive you. And I don't have a plan." The two sat in silence for a while. Mark had begun to think that they would be going back to the pleasant silence before Lincoln continued.

"I have one now. We get our own, irrefutable proof that the mayor is corrupt. We will spread this around town anonymously. He will get in trouble and lose his credibility. The plan would a success."

"H–hang on." Mark shook his head. "You serious?" Lincoln nodded.

"How... would we even go about that?"

"You'll hate it."

Mark groaned.

The mayor's house was three stories tall and had clearly stood the test of time– with its thin, worn walls painted in faded colors, Mark half thought that it would vanish into dust if a light breeze swept through the air. At the same time, with the way it towered over him, Mark felt intimidated at the same time.

"No one is awake," Lincoln murmured. "Let's be careful."

With a swallow, Mark donned his ski mask. "You talk me into the weirdest crap..." He muttered.

Clad in the same outfits they had worn when interrogating Arnie, the two carefully trekked through the picturesque gardens surrounding the house- Mark could see that, even in the dead of night, the dewy grass seemed to shine.

When they got to the door, Lincoln turned to him. "Pick the lock now." He instructed in a low voice.

Mark obliged, and with a swift movement, he stuck a pair of bobby pins in the lock and manipulated them until the door opened with a click. The two quickly slipped in, Lincoln closing the door behind them.

The lights were off, and Mark pulled out a flashlight- a tiny little thing that could fit inside his fist. He clicked it on, and once his eyes adjusted to the light, he examined his surroundings.

In front of them, there was a grand staircase. Mark unconsciously started towards it before Lincoln stopped him.

"I'll go to the next floor," Lincoln said.

"Oh. Uh... okay–"

Before he could finish his response, Lincoln stuck his hand out to Mark. In one hand, he held a roll of black masking tape, and in the other, he held two small, similarly colored chips.

"These are the audio bugs," He whispered, shifting the hand that held the chips up. "Hide these two in two separate locations on the first floor, using the tape if needed. I will now go to the second floor and do the same with the other bugs."

Mark nodded, taking the chips and the roll of tape, before scurrying away, his heartbeat ringing in his ears.

He headed to the right of the staircase, where there was a hallway lined with paintings. He saw one that was of a pink spiral, and lifted it slightly off the wall by its corner. With his free hand, he slipped a bug out of his pocket and pinned it to the wall, before taping it up and setting the painting back in place, the bug now obscured.

The hallway on the other side of the staircase had plenty of paintings as well, so he did the same with a painting of a lattice of green and black. He quickly made his way back to the stairs, standing at the bottom step as he waited for Lincoln.

After a few moments, Lincoln walked back down the stairs, moving to stand next to him.

"The bugs may pick up something incriminating, which will get sent to my computer. Then, we can anonymously distribute the audio."

Mark nodded.

Then, he felt his blood run cold when he heard a door creak open.

"*Shit.*" Mark hissed, his heart skipping a beat.

He was prepared to run before he felt Lincoln's hand grasp his. Unceremoniously, he was dragged behind a ridiculously large potted plant, bigger than the two of them combined. Crouching, the two were now obscured. Through the leaves and stems of the plant, he watched a light click on from upstairs, illuminating the bottom floor, and he saw a figure trudging down the stairs.

Axel.

Mark watched him rub his eyes as he walked downstairs, heading into the hallway to the right.

Mark took a minute to breathe before he saw Axel walking back, now clutching a glass of water.

He had just begun to start back up the stairs when Mark heard a series of footsteps thumping against the ground, growing louder as they grew closer.

An obscenely large, middle-aged man, clad in a bathrobe, walked down the stairs, stopping to frown down at Axel.

"That's the mayor," Lincoln whispered, and Mark felt his blood spike.

"The hell are you doing?" The mayor asked, in a low, raspy, but unmistakably threatening voice.

"I was getting water–"

"I told you not to leave your room at night."

Axel rolled his eyes. "I was thirsty–"

"Don't *roll your eyes* at me."

"Oh, *fuck* you–"

There was a slam and a shattering. It happened fast enough that Mark only registered what had happened when he saw the aftermath. The cup Axel was holding lay in pieces on the floor, a puddle of water under and around the broken glass. Axel had flinched away from the mayor, whose hand was out, palm facing down toward the mess on the floor. For a moment, there was a truly savage look in the mayor's eyes, but it flickered away in favor of something colder, more controlled.

"Show some damn respect." He said, stepping over the broken glass, advancing toward Axel. "This is *my* house. The least you could do is *try* to follow the rules."

Axel snorted. "*Your* house? The *town* paid for–"

The mayor drove a fist into Axel's stomach, hard enough that he was knocked onto the ground. Slowly sitting up, he glared up at the mayor, hatred swirling in his eyes.

It was subtler, but Mark also saw the pain in them.

"Get to bed." The mayor barked.

Axel sat on the ground for a long moment, before finally standing, trudging up the staircase. The mayor followed him.

As Mark stared after him, Lincoln tapped his shoulder. "We should go." He said, quietly.

Numbly, Mark nodded in response.

"Wait, wait, start over." Ellie shook her head, before frowning at Mark and Lincoln, who sat across the table. "You broke into the mayor's house to plant some bugs. Both of you went, so... why didn't you call me?"

"It would've been tougher to break in. With three people. And we...we kinda forgot. About you." Mark said, looking down, feeling a bit red.

"...Ouch. Okay." Ellie leaned back in her seat. "...so... what happened next? Did you get the bugs in?"

"We planted four of them, two on each floor," Lincoln replied, not looking up at either of them.

Mark nodded, before staring down at his hands, wrung together on the table. "And... we also saw something. I... I don't..."

"Mayor Warner abuses Axel." Lincoln cut him off.

Mark winced, and Ellie stared at Lincoln, incredulous.

"What... what are you talking about?"

"We saw him shout at him and assault him." He replied, fidgeting his hands in one another.

"I..." Ellie stared down at her lap. "I... are you sure?"

"I saw it, so yes, I am sure."

The three sat in silence for a moment after that.

"I... what do we do with that?" Mark asked, hushed. "We... tell someone? Or..."

Lincoln looked up at the ceiling before he finally spoke. "Perhaps. This could be the 'something incriminating' we were looking for."

Mark slowly turned to look at Lincoln. "Wait... are you saying we–" When Mark cut himself off, Lincoln finished his question for him.

"We reveal the fact that he is an abusive father to the public eye? The answer is yes."

"*Wait.*" Mark furrowed his brows. "I... where's the proof? I mean, we–"

"The bugs were recording at the time. The proof is in my computer."

Mark stared at Lincoln before he began to stammer. "I– but... *should* we tell anyone?"

"Mayor Warner's reputation would be ruined."

"Well, yeah, but..." Mark shifted against the cushioning of his seat. "I... if he's really hitting him, or... we– we might– we– maybe we shouldn't tell anyone. We... we're just gonna tell everyone this guy was hitting his kid? I..." Mark trailed off.

"But this way, he'd get his comeuppance. Why–" Lincoln's eyes comically widened in realization. "You feel sympathy for Axel."

"What? No. I– that's..." Mark trailed off.

He let himself escape mentally for a moment before he spoke again. "I... maybe. My old foster parents... I told you how they were. A–and now... Axel's getting..."

"I understand how you feel. But please keep in mind that Axel is a violent sociopath who physically assaulted both of us and summoned a demon that killed two people."

Mark sharply turned to Lincoln, glaring at him. "I *know that*, dumbass. But... it–" Mark released a heavy sigh. "I *know*, he's a jackass. But I wouldn't want the whole town knowing about... you know, on someone else's terms, so... I just..."

"Okay. I get it." Lincoln nodded, though it seemed it was more for himself than Mark. "We will not use this information if we come up with something else from the bugs."

Mark hummed in response, but Ellie chimed in.

"*Wait*. Are... are we gonna do anything?" Ellie asked, her voice a bit hoarse. "I mean, this kid's getting abused. I... I hate Axel, but... I..."

Mark shook his head. "Ellie, I get it, and... but I don't think we can really do anything. I mean... we can't call the cops, or anything like that. But... when we release all the info, we... he'll get taken away. So... yeah."

Slowly, Ellie nodded, seeming slightly placated. "...okay. Y-yeah. That... that makes sense. Yeah."

It was then that Lincoln began to drum his fingers on the table, seeming fascinated by the thumps he made against the polished wood. He kept at it for a long few moments before stopping and pressing his hands down against the table, hard enough that Mark could see the edges of his hands turn white.

"Don't take this the wrong way. We do not have the whole story." Lincoln started, not looking up at Mark or Ellie.

Mark cocked his head. "What do you mean?"

"Mayor Warner's an awful person, considering the coverups, but think about Axel. And his personality." Lincoln pursed his lips before he continued. "He may not be an innocent victim in this. Maybe he is just as awful to his father as he is to him."

Mark stared at Lincoln. "I- yeah... but..."

The pained look on Axel's face flashed in his mind.

"I... we don't know." Ellie conceded. "But... but that doesn't mean he can just hit his kid!"

Lincoln nodded. "You're right- it doesn't."

The next day was also a day off.

Today, Ellie had invited Mark to come over to her house. He agreed, but as he walked through the neighborhood where she lived, he felt hundreds of second thoughts creeping up on him.

It was clear that this neighborhood alone had more money than half the world's countries. He trekked through a land of pristine, modernist architecture, staring at the ground he walked on as he tried not to look up.

Eventually, when Maps had alerted him that he was at Ellie's, he looked up to face a gorgeous villa, the sound of a fountain pouring water into itself filling his ears.

Reluctantly, he walked up to the door and rang the bell.

After a few minutes, Ellie came to the door, with a wide grin.

"Hey, Mark! Come in!"

Mark followed Ellie inside, where he was greeted by the scent of melted butter. Ellie turned a corner, and led him into a large kitchen. On the stove, there was a heated pan, filled to the brim with popcorn kernels.

"I always liked kettle more than microwaved," Ellie laughed as they began to pop. Once the popcorn was ready, she dumped the pan out into a large bowl.

"So!" She said, holding the bowl in her hands. "I was thinking we could watch a movie! You got anything in mind?" Mark shrugged. "Whatever you got, I guess."

"Well, we got pretty much everything. My dad's a TV junkie, so we have, like, 99% of all the streaming services. And, like, a thousand DVDs."

Mark cocked an eyebrow. "DVDs...? I– whatever. Anything's fine."

Ellie hummed, glancing down at the ground. "Anything...?"

"Sure."

"...Can we watch Pink Princess?"

Mark stared blankly at her. "*What.*"

Pink Princess was an infamous children's movie. Mark had never seen it, but it was known for being obscenely saccharine and cutesy.

"Don't– it's good, *okay*?" Ellie said, defensive. It was as if she could read Mark's mind. Glancing away, she sheepishly continued. "I– we don't *have* to... but..."

Seeing the look on her face, Mark took pity on her.

"...okay. Sure."

Ellie *beamed.*

Leaning back on the couch, stuffing a handful of popcorn into his mouth, Mark admitted to himself that the movie was actually really good.

The art and animation were clearly drawn with love and skill. The characters were all funny, and they worked well together. Mark liked the plot, even if it was a little cliched.

As he cringed at himself for thinking like a pretentious movie critic, he heard Ellie mutter something inaudible.

He turned to her, but before he could ask, he saw from the way her lips moved that she was mouthing along with the movie. Enthusiastically so, if the grin on her face was anything to go by.

Mark stared at her for a moment, before smirking and turning back to the screen.

When the movie ended, Ellie stared at the rolling credits for a good few minutes, before smiling to herself, patting the cushions on the couch until she found the remote.

"God, I forgot how good that was." Ellie breathed, giggling a bit.

"It… it was actually pretty okay." Mark conceded.

"Pretty *okay*? It's a *masterpiece!*" Ellie grinned manically, and Mark cocked his head at her.

"Whatever you say." He said, smiling wryly as he looked down at the floor.

"...Ship anyone?" Ellie asked, mischievously.

"Pink Princess and Green Princess," Mark replied without hesitation. Then he realized what he had just answered. "Wait, *what?*"

Ellie giggled, before shaking her head. "But Pink's a lot cuter with Purple!"

"I- *moving on,*" Mark quickly tried to change the subject. "What... do you want to do something else now?"

Ellie hummed, slumping her back onto the couch. "I dunno. Maybe talk? Finish the popcorn?" She gestured at the half-eaten bowl.

Mark nodded. "Okay. Yeah, we can do that."

The two slouched on the couch, sharing dumb jokes and petty insults with one another. Mark made a petty comment about Ellie's dye job, and in response she said something so outrageously obscene that the two were sent into a fit of uncontrollable laughter. Wiping tears from his eyes, Mark checked his watch.

"Gotta leave in a few," He murmured, a bit dejected.

Ellie pouted. "Shoot."

Mark stretched, standing up with Ellie. "Uh... by the way, just curious, where's your parents? Didn't see them."

Ellie blinked, before grimacing. "They're in Hawaii."

"...why?" Mark asked dumbly.

"Vacation." Ellie glared at the floor.

"And... they didn't bring you?"

Ellie gave a curt shake of her head.

"... Oh. That- that sucks." Mark scratched at the back of his neck, feeling uncomfortably sympathetic.

Ellie was quiet for a bit before she spoke again. "I... they do this a lot. I... I guess they don't wanna spend time with me. I know, I know, *news flash*." She finished with a bitter chuckle, before looking up at Mark, regretful. "I- I'm sorry. This is kinda dumb. You can go. It was nice seeing you."

Before he could say anything, Ellie led Mark out to the front door, practically dragging him along.

"Okay, yeah. I'll see you at school–" Ellie tried to close the door on him, but Mark spoke first.

"*Wait.*" He breathed. Ellie stopped to look at him with her lips parted, the door only part-way closed.

Mark blanched a little when he realized that he didn't know what to say to Ellie at that moment. "I... you're good. You're a good kid, Ellie."

Ellie raised an eyebrow. "We're the same age, Mark–"

"You should be in Hawaii, right now. Not... not here. Not in this town. With... with the demons and..." Mark trailed off, embarrassment finally catching up to him.

But his discomfort cooled when he saw Ellie's gaze soften before she gave him a small smile.

"Thanks, Mark." Mark awkwardly cracked a smile at her before she closed the door on him.

Mark: *you want to talk about what happened*
Even though he saw that Ellie had read the message, nearly half an hour passed before she responded.
Ellie: *okay.*
Another minute passed.
Ellie: *can i vent?*
Mark: *yeah.*
Mark: *go ahead.*
Mark saw that Ellie was typing, but it took a long moment before she sent the message.

Ellie: *my parents always leave me at the house. and they never really spend time with me. sometimes i dont see them for weeks, and they dont answer my calls. i feel like theyre ignoring me.*

Ellie: *i KNOW, they love me and I love them, and I know im overreacting, but i wish they'd stay at home.*

Mark: *fuck no.*

Mark: *you're not overreacting.*

Mark: *your parents are dicks for that. youre their kid. they cant just randomly go on vacation without you*

Ellie: *dicks? really?*

Ellie: *its not THAT bad*

Ellie: *i get the house to myself, and they leave a lot of money for groceries.*

Mark: *still not okay*

Mark: *look i grew up in a lot of shitty houses.*

Ellie: *wait.*

Ellie: *this is NOT as bad as that*

Ellie: *you had it awful*

Ellie: *and my parents just go on a lot of trips. Thats not the same thing*

Mark: *well yeah*

Mark: *but its still shitty*

Ellie: *i get where youre coming from*

Ellie: *but they really aren't that bad, i SWEAR*

Ellie: *thanks, though, for saying something*

Mark: *...you're welcome, ig*

Neither of them sent anything for a while after that.

Ellie: *pink and green? seriously?*

Mark: NO. *im not talking about that.*

Ellie: *come on! I just wanna know why*

Mark: NO

Ellie: *pleeaase?*

Mark: *will it get you off my back if I say something?*

Ellie: *yeah!*

Mark: *they stuck around for each other when they needed it. it was cute. Happy?*

Now and before, Mark felt nothing but regret and embarrassment for dignifying Ellie's questions with answers.

Ellie: *aww*

Ellie: *knew you were a softie*

Mark: SHUT UP

Mark: *its midnight. go to bed*

Ellie: *Love you too, Mark. Night!*

Mark: *night*

Chuckling to himself, Mark switched his phone off and curled up into bed.

Mark was walking through the halls when he felt a hand clasp his shoulder.

"Hey, Mark?"

He turned to face Daisy, a chubby, pasty girl from his world history class. Knowing her irritating but genuine sunny personality, Mark let his guard down, convinced she didn't want any trouble.

"Can I talk to you, for a moment?" She asked shyly.

Mark glanced around before nodding.

Daisy nodded. "This morning, when I was walking to school... I ran into this girl. She looked... kinda crazy... but she kept saying she was looking for someone, and- and she could've meant a different Mark, but..." She looked down at her shoes. "Is your last name Langley?"

Mark narrowed his eyes. "Yeah, it is. Who..."

At that moment, something clicked in his head.

"Did you get her name?"

Daisy shook her head.

"Okay, what'd she look like?"

"Well... she had this messy red hair-"

Rita.

"Where'd you see her?"

"Uh... the corner of Park and Chester. Why-"

Mark immediately excused himself from the conversation.

School had just ended, and people began to pool out the doors. After leaving the school, pulling his phone out, he texted Rick.

Mark: *meeting up with a friend. ill be home by curfew*

Rick: *Okay.*

Slipping his phone back in his pocket, he had begun to start toward the Park-Chester area, when, from a few yards away, his eyes locked with Axel's.

He saw him smirk and advance towards him. Out of instinct, Mark stood upright, looking away from him.

"Hey, jackass." Axel gave him a grin wide enough that Mark could see the back rows of his teeth.

For a long moment, Mark could only stare at Axel.

He'd been avoiding him like the plague ever since he talked to Alita. This was the first time in several days that he'd looked directly at Axel, and now, he saw a multitude of things.

He saw the boy that had gotten people killed. The boy that had hurt him and his friends. The boy whose dad had hurt him, and had looked so pained afterward. It was impossible to reconcile it all.

"...Why- why are you looking at me like that-?"

Mark stepped back, before he began sprinting as fast as he could from the scene. He'd gotten strange looks, and he was exhausted and out of breath, but after a few minutes, Axel was nowhere near him.

This wasn't the time. He should be focusing on stopping Lila.

Letting his breaths settle back to normal, Mark began to travel to the streets where Daisy had seen Rita.

"There you are!"

Recognizing the familiar voice, he turned around to face Rita, who was running up to him.

"I've been looking for you all day, fuck!" She glared at him as if this was somehow his fault.

"Wait, wait." Mark shook his head. "Why are you *here*? You live in Riverside."

"Wow, figured that out on your own, genius?" Rita sneered at him. "I came to help you guys. See if you managed to figure something out."

"I- oh." Mark nodded. "We... we actually looked through your notes, and we figured out how to stop her."

"Really?" Rita gaped a bit at him. "*How?*"

Mark described the page that Lincoln had found, telling her about their plan.

"So... you're just gonna drug him?" Rita cocked an eyebrow.

"Y-yeah. Basically." Mark looked down at the ground.

"Sounds risky." Rita drawled.

"We don't have a better idea." Mark snapped.

Rita hummed for a bit. "Sounds like you guys are gonna need some help."

Mark frowned, looking back up. "What... what're you getting at?"

"I'm *saying*," Rita crossed her arms over her chest, "That I'm gonna be in town for a week, cause of all this. I can help you with your plan."

Mark blinked. "I... in town? For a week?"

Rita rolled her eyes. "What are you, deaf?"

Mark glared at her, before shaking his head. "Wait, what about Alita? Who's gonna–"

"Neighbor owed me a favor. She's looking after her while I'm gone. I'm staying at that Motel 6 a couple of blocks back. So... can I help you guys?"

Mark stared at her for a moment, before nodding. "Okay."

"Good. Also, can I get your number? Cause this really could've been over a phone call."

Reluctantly, Mark exchanged numbers with the hot-headed girl before heading back to Rick's house.

Back at their booth in the diner, the trio, plus Rita, fleshed out their plan.

Checking lunar calendars online, they confirmed tomorrow would be the day Lila would possess Axel.

Throughout the morning and the afternoon, they'd keep a close eye on Axel. Considering the fact that the book had specified '*the last quarter of the day*,' he probably wouldn't get possessed during the day, but they'd follow him around just in case, and they'd stop him from hurting anyone, if necessary.

Then, assuming he wasn't yet possessed, they'd slip Axel a note telling him to meet in an abandoned house that was relatively close to Ellie's.

They'd drug him, take him to Ellie's basement, and tie him up. Once he was possessed, they'd force-feed him the gallons of holy water Ellie had bought.

Then, they'd be able to go back to their lives.

"Can't believe we're gonna save the world..." Ellie laughed, breathlessly.

Rita snorted. "You know, there's a pretty big chance this could go completely wrong, and we'll all die."

Ellie pouted at her before Lincoln spoke up.

"It's either we might save the world, or we might not, or we definitely don't save the world, and we definitely all die." A bit wryly, Lincoln smiled down at the table. "I think the latter's an upgrade. Ladders go up."

Raising an eyebrow, Rita opened her mouth and closed it.

"Whatever. I'm hungry. Spot me."

Mark frowned. "...Why?"

"I'm broke. Spent it all at the hotel."

Scoffing, Mark narrowed his eyes. "Why should we–"

"Hey, I drove four hours for this!" Mark rolled his eyes.

"Here you go." Lincoln fished through his pocket, pulling out a wrinkled twenty.

Waving a waiter over, she ordered a bowl of mac and cheese, and the waiter quickly brought it over. She practically inhaled the dish.

"So, I'm gonna head back to the motel," She said, gulping down one last mouthful of mac and cheese. "Thanks for the food."

Springing up, she left the diner.

"*God*," Mark scoffed.

Ellie shook her head. "Okay... that was not cool!"

Lincoln nodded vigorously. "It was the exact opposite of cool. It was hot."

Mark and Ellie slowly turned to face Lincoln.

"What is it?" Lincoln's eyes widened. "Oh. That came out wrong."

"That your type, Lincoln?" Ellie said, snorting.

Lincoln narrowed his eyes. "My type is men. So no."

Ellie blinked. "Shit, okay. Anyway–"

"*Wait*. What?" Mark choked out.

Lincoln raised an eyebrow. "I said, I'm attracted to men. Exclusively. I am gay."

"...Oh."

Some men liked men. That was no secret to anyone, least of all to Mark. And yet, the revelation made Mark's head reel, and all he could do was stare at Lincoln owlishly.

"Is there a problem with that, Mark?" Lincoln asked with narrowed eyes.

"What? No! I–" Mark shook his head, quickly sobering. "Sorry. I was just surprised."

"I thought so."

"I– uh..." Mark looked away from Lincoln. "I'm bi."

Lincoln stared at him for a long moment, his gaze softening. "Oh."

"Y–yeah."

Lincoln kept staring at him, while Mark avoided eye contact.

"Thank you for telling me."

"R–right."

Mark finally met Lincoln's eyes, and suddenly, he was vividly aware of Lincoln's soft build, his pale skin, his hundreds of freckles.

"*Um*," Ellie said, clearing her throat. "Not to sound insensitive or whatever, but your guys' dating life isn't really a pressing issue right now."

Mark shook his head out of his stupor. "Right. *Moving on*," Mark cleared his throat. "Your house, right?" He asked, turning to Ellie, who nodded.

"Yep. My parents are still out, so sneaking you guys down shouldn't be too hard!" She gave them a smile, before letting out a long breath.

"I guess... we just gotta get some rest tonight. Get ready for tomorrow." Mark and Lincoln nodded at this. With a long breath, Mark leaned back in the seat.

"Okay. Yeah. Lincoln, you got the chloroform ready?"

At that moment, a waitress passing by froze, gawking at them.

He and the waitress stared blankly at one another for a good few moments.

"*Chlorine.*" Mark choked out. "Sorry. You got the *chlorine* ready? For the... pool."

The almost certainly unconvinced waitress walked away.

"The chlorine is ready." Lincoln finally replied.

"You can't just say that in public!" Ellie cried.

Mark threw his hands up. "We've been talking about drugging this guy for half an hour!"

"Let's find a new meetup place," Lincoln said, glancing around the diner.

They left the diner soon after that.

Ellie had said goodbye and left for her house, leaving Mark and Lincoln standing in front of the diner.

"It's getting warmer," Mark said, glancing up at the sky.

Lincoln fidgeted a bit with his hands. "Is that a metaphor? For us finally putting an end to this?"

"Wha– no. It– it's literally getting warmer. It's like... ten degrees warmer than yesterday."

"...oh," Lincoln said. "Sorry."

"Don't say sorry if you didn't do anything wrong."

"Okay."

The two stood side by side in silence for a moment. The only sound in the air was the light breeze whistling.

"Mark?"

"Yeah?"

"I'm scared."

Mark turned to look at Lincoln, who was staring at the ground.

"I... of what?" He asked lamely.

"I'm scared the chloroform might not work. I'm scared the holy water might not work. I'm scared that we might get in trouble. I'm scared that we could all *die*."

In the two weeks that he knew him, Mark never heard Lincoln sound so pained.

He hated it.

"I..." Mark paused, unsure of what to say. "I get it. I'm scared too." With a sigh, Mark stared up at the evening sky.

"I...I *know* this is risky. If this doesn't work, we're all gonna die. But..." Mark rubbed the bridge of his nose, before looking back at Lincoln. "We gotta try. If– if we don't then... we're definitely not gonna make it." He turned back to Lincoln, who was staring ahead, a typical, unreadable expression on his face. "I... you know that, don't you?"Lincoln was inanimate for a long moment before he nodded. "I do. I knew all of this." Lincoln met Mark's eyes, and he gave him a small smile. "I just wanted to hear it from you."

"From me," Mark repeated. Lincoln nodded. "You wanted advice. From me." Wryly, he pointed at himself.

"Yes, because you're my friend and I look up to you."

Mark stared at Lincoln for a minute, before he shook his head, laughing a bit.

"I am being serious, you know."

"I know, I know you are, it's just..." Mark rubbed the back of his neck. "You... you give me too much credit." Mark vaguely gestured at himself. "I- I'm kind of a shitshow, man."

"Oh. Don't worry- I am too."

Mark laughed a bit, smiling down at himself.

"I... seriously, though. I think we'll be okay. We'll get through this. The plan. And... and I don't think I'm wrong."

Lincoln blinked at him, before glancing away. "Thank you, Mark." He whispered.

Staring at Lincoln, an impulse began to creep into his head. With a quickened heartbeat, Mark gently took hold of Lincoln's hand, running the tip of his thumb down the back of it.

For a moment, Lincoln didn't do anything, but just as Mark had begun to panic and tried to pull his hand away, Lincoln lightly squeezed it.

They stood like that for a moment, clutching each other's hands as they faced forward, Mark not having it in him to look Lincoln in the eye. A delightfully feverish sensation overtook him, and Mark was desperate not to ruin it, terrified into stillness by the mere prospect.

With a swallow, Mark finally spoke. "I... is this okay?"

In the corner of his eye, he could see Lincoln nod. "Yes." He said, not looking at him.

Mark didn't know how long they had been standing there, before he hoarsely excused himself and went back to his house, the warmth of Lincoln's hand still lingering on his own.

"Are you guys ready for this?" Ellie asked Mark and Lincoln, who both nodded in reply.

They were waiting in a dark corner of the abandoned house, knowing that it was only a matter of minutes before Axel showed up.

"You got the rag ready, right?" Ellie asked, nodding at Lincoln.

He held up the damp, sweet-smelling rag that Mark wisely scooted away from.

"So... you're just gonna run up behind him and..." Mark slammed his hand over his mouth and nose, miming the action he'd seen in action movies.

"Yes, but it's not that simple," Lincoln said, glancing down at the ground. "Chloroform could take–"

The three of them collectively froze when they heard a door creak open, before slamming shut behind him.

"Hey!" A voice that was unmistakably Axel's called out. "What's–" Lincoln acted quickly, running out the corner, and taking a turn into the hall where he heard the call. Mark and Ellie quickly followed, making it out just in time to see Lincoln jump onto Axel, clamping the rag over his mouth.

Axel let out a muffled scream as he writhed, trying to overpower Lincoln, and clearly about to succeed.

"Help!" Lincoln shouted.

Immediately, Mark and Ellie ran over, pinning down Axel's arms and legs.

"Why is he still awake!?" Ellie cried.

"Contrary to popular belief, chloroform can take about five minutes to fully drive someone unconscious."

Mark cursed to himself, grunting with effort as Axel violently thrashed under him. Finally, after a few minutes, Axel went still.

Slowly moving away from him, the three stood upright.

"*Oh my god,*" Ellie breathed, cupping her hands over her mouth. "We just *drugged* someone."

"And now we are going to kidnap him." Lincoln ran back to the corner, and came back with a large bag, unrolling so that it was long enough to squeeze Axel inside.

Silently, the three carefully loaded his still body into the bag, zipping it up when they were done. On the count of three, they lifted Axel up, each of them grunting in unison, before carrying him over to Ellie's house.

A couple of passersby had given them strange looks, but none of them indicated that they knew there was a person inside the bag.

After an exhausting few minutes, they finally made their way into Ellie's cellar. They practically dropped the bag on the floor, each of them panting and wheezing.

"Tie him up," Lincoln nodded to Mark, who unzipped the bag, pulling it out from under Axel, leaving his body lying on the floor.

"Do you have a rope, Ellie?"

She ran to the back of the cellar, rummaging a bit through a bin before pulling out a thick rolled-up rope.

"Tie him to that." Ellie said, pointing at a concrete column in the center of the basement.

Nodding, Mark dragged Axel to the column, forcing his body to sit upright, and tying the rope around him and the column as tightly as he possibly could.

Panting a little, Mark looked between Ellie and Lincoln before crouching down on the cold ground.

"Rita still coming?" He asked from the floor.

Lincoln nodded. "Yes. It should only be a matter of time before she gets here."

As if on cue, he heard a distant knocking. Ellie ran up the stairs out of the cellar, and after a few minutes, came back with Rita trailing behind her.

"You couldn't have helped us with this?" Mark glared at her, gesturing at Axel.

"I was busy. Be happy I came at all." After Rita made her way down the stairs, she walked around Axel's body, scrutinizing it. "So this is the mayor's kid, huh?"

"Yes. He will awaken in a couple of hours, and subsequently be possessed by Rita."

Rita hummed. "So... we're just waiting around?"

"Yep," Ellie said, stretching.

"Do... do we have to stay in here?" Raising an eyebrow, Rita looked around the cellar. "This place is kinda depressing."

Ellie frowned. "I... I guess not, but... we can't just leave him," She nodded at Axel. "But I don't wanna stay down here, either."

Lincoln chimed in at that. "We could take one-hour shifts. And one stays down, and the rest go up."

Mark hummed. "Okay... but who's gonna go first?"

After a beat of silence, Ellie and Rita put their fingers on their noses. After another beat, Lincoln did the same.

"I...I hate you guys." He said, defeated.

After an hour in the basement, aimlessly checking his phone, he perked up when he heard the basement door creak open.

Looking up the stairs, he turned to see Lincoln standing in the doorframe, looking down at him.

Mark stared dumbly at him for a long moment. It was the first time since yesterday at the diner that they were alone together, and the air was immediately filled with a painful awkwardness, as he recalled the borderline intimate moment they'd shared.

"Oh... uh, hey." Rubbing the back of his neck, Mark rushed up the stairs so that he was facing Lincoln.

Lincoln wouldn't look at him. "Hello." He nodded.

"I... I guess it's your turn now?" Mark gestured to the bottom of the stairs.

"Yes." Lincoln started down the staircase, not saying another word.

...Oh.

Mark slumped over, the inside of his chest crumbling with regret at what he'd done the other night.

"Uh, yeah. I'll, I'll see you when you're... done." Mark looked down at Lincoln for a moment, biting at the inside of his cheek.

Real smooth, Langley. Mark shook his head, before walking out the door and shutting it behind him.

"God," He heard a familiar cackle. "That was *painful.*"

Mark whipped his head around to face Rita, who leaned against the wall as she smirked at him.

"I– *shut up.*" He said, glaring at her.

She laughed in response. "Like *Jesus,* I never saw a guy get that obvious. I almost feel bad–"

"What– what the *hell's* your problem?!"

Mark nearly blew out his throat when he screamed that at Rita, but he couldn't care less. Who the *hell* did this girl think she was?

Vaguely satisfied by how taken aback she looked, he kept yelling. "E–Ever since you got here, you've been acting awful! *The fuck* is your damage?" Mark glared at Rita, who snarled back at him.

"Oh, I'm sorry, I'm not all sunshine and rainbows!" Rita sprung away from the wall, advancing toward him. "My aunt's getting worse, I have to help you guys, and if this shit doesn't work out, the world's gonna *fucking* end!"

Mark opened his mouth to yell again, but he immediately stopped when he saw the tears that were threatening to spill out of Rita's eyes. Angrily, she wiped them away.

"I..." Mark started lamely. "You... *you're scared.*" Mark breathed.

Rita flinched as if she had been scalded. "What? No! I– I'm not..." Rita looked down, grumbling something inaudible.

"Fine. You got me. I'm *scared*, that we– that I– might fuck this up. Happy?" She said, with a slight hiss.

Mark shook his head. "I... yeah. So are we. We all are. I... I get it."

Rita rolled her eyes. "Right."

"...I'm serious–"

"Yeah, *I know you are.*" Rita sharply cut him off.

There was a long silence in the air after that, and Mark picked at his fingernails to try and distract himself from it.

"Fine." Rita finally said curtly.

Mark raised an eyebrow. "Fine... what?"

"I'll shut up. Stop being a bitch, all of that, until we get this done." Rita nodded, though it was clearly more directed at herself than Mark.

"I... good." He awkwardly replied, after a pause.

"...I... I'm just kinda..." Rita scoffed a bit, staring at the floor. "It's easier to be mean than nice. To deal with everything." Mark took a sharp breath, the familiarity of Rita's words sending a chill down his back.

"I... yeah. I get that." Mark played with a strand of his hair, careful not to look directly at Rita. "I... when I was a kid, I never really trusted or liked anyone. So... it was better, just to... kinda act like a dick. It got people to go away. But..." Mark chuckled to himself. "I... I was miserable. It... it really didn't help things, in the end. You..." Mark trailed off and looked up at Rita.

"I... yeah. That makes sense." Nodding to herself, she walked away, likely heading to the kitchen, before she stopped in her tracks.

"...Thanks." She said quietly. Then she kept walking.

A couple hours later, just before Ellie was supposed to go, Mark found himself back in the basement, checking on Axel's body.

It'd only be a matter of time before Lila possessed him. It'd probably be even less time before Axel woke up.

He heard Ellie knocking on the door upstairs.

With a grunt, he stood up and began to start up the staircase, when he heard a long groan from behind him.

"What... where am I?" A voice slurred.

Mark whipped around to stare at Axel, who was blinking his eyes open. He screamed for the others to come down.

"What... Mark?" Having regained his bearings, Axel whipped his head over to stare at him. "*What the fuck is this!?*" He tried to stand, but to no avail, and he looked down at the rope that bound him. "*Why the hell am I tied up!?*"

At that, the door burst open, and Lincoln, Ellie, and Rita came running down the stairs.

"He's awake!" Ellie yelped.

"Did– did you fucking *drug me? What the* HELL!?" He thrashed against the rope, but it held strong against him.

"LET ME GO, YOU FUCKING PSYCHOS! I'LL FUCKING KILL YOU!"Axel kept screaming obscenities at the top of his lungs.

"*Fuck*, this is annoying…" Rita pinched the bridge of her nose.

"I will make him stop." Lincoln took his backpack off his shoulders, and, rummaging through it, he pulled out a cloth and a roll of duct tape. Balling the cloth up, he quickly ran over to Axel, shoving it into his mouth, despite his violent protests. Before he could spit it out, in a swift movement, Lincoln pulled a length of tape off the roll and wrapped it over his mouth, before tearing it off. When he stepped away, Axel's screams were completely muffled.

"He is quieter now," Lincoln said, with a completely unearned casualness.

Slowly, Rita eyed Lincoln, looking impressed. "Damn, I underestimated you."

"Many do."

Axel let out a long shriek that chilled Mark, even with the gag.

"Okay… Axel," Ellie started. "We can explain. But you gotta calm down. You'll be fine, we'll probably be abe to let you go in a few hours, but we *need* you to calm down."Axel stared at Ellie incredulously, breathing hard.

"Nod, if you get it."

Axel furiously glared at Ellie, but after a moment, with a clear reluctance, he nodded.

"Okay. We're gonna tell you *everything*. Why you're here. Got it?"

Once more, Axel nodded.

"...And then, we brought you here." Mark finished.

After a few moments of silence from Axel, Lincoln walked over to him and ripped the gag off.

Spitting out the cloth, Axel was quiet for a few more seconds, before he finally spoke.

"You're... you're *fucking* kidding." He let out an empty cackle. "You *people*, you're... you're fucking *psychos*!" Axel snarled. "I mean, yeah, I was looking around the library. Yeah, I- I found the book, and I did the spell! But- but there's *no way* in *hell* I got fucking POSSESSED!"

Silently, the four of them looked at each other.

"Axel," Lincoln said quietly. "If you insist on your innocence, then tell us what you were doing on the nights of the deaths of Eric Jacobs and Nina Cristen."

Axel opened his mouth to say something, but he slowly closed it, a look of unmistakable horror dawning on his face.

"I... I don't remember." He said, weakly.

"I- I- *no*. I didn't do it." Axel stammered. "I... I *didn't*. I didn't kill those people. I *didn't*."

"Are you trying to convince us, or yourself?" Lincoln asked, hushed.

At that, Axel froze. Then, his face began to twist into a manic grin.

"I- it's my fault." He said, beginning to cackle hoarsely. "All just because... *because I-*" Then, his expression fell right back into agony.

"Fuck. I... *I killed them.*" He whispered.

He stared at the ground, and Mark felt as if he was waiting for a bomb to be set off.

"...Get it out of me." Axel rasped.

"...What-?"

"GET IT THE FUCK OUT OF ME!" Axel shrieked. "I'M NOT GONNA BE FUCKING POSSESSED! I HATE THIS- I-"

"AXEL!" Lincoln shouted, loud enough that everybody in the room stilled, even Axel. Lincoln continued in a normal tone of voice. "I would like to remind you that we have a plan to get rid of the demon. And we will enact it in a few hours. But I ask you, *please* be patient." Axel went quiet for a moment, before the fear faded from his face, and he sneered at Lincoln.

"You're sick in the head, you know that?" Axel smirked, but looking at it, Mark could see how hollow the look on his face really was.

"*Moving on,*" Ellie said, clearing her throat. "Can someone grab the holy water? There's four gallons, so... maybe two people, carrying two each?"

At that moment, Ellie and Rita put their fingers on their noses.

Mark and Lincoln, whose noses were very much untouched, turned to look at each other.

Why the hell am I so slow? Mark thought, ruefully.

The walk upstairs was painfully awkward.

Mark and Lincoln didn't say a word to each other until they got to the table where Ellie had put the holy water. Mark and Lincoln each grabbed two of the jugs by their handles, and they started back toward the cellar. But halfway there, Mark heard a loud bang, he whipped his head around.

Apparently, Lincoln had dropped a jug, and though he was bending over to pick it up, it was rolling over to Mark, so, instinctively, he reached down, setting one of his own jugs down, picking it up, and handing it to Lincoln.

Slowly, Lincoln reached out and took it, his fingers brushing his as he took hold of the handle.

"Thank you." He said quietly.

"...yeah."

A deafening silence hung in the air, and Mark felt that he had to say something. "Uh... listen, I– I know this is a really bad time, but about the other day... I... I'm sorry, I'm not sure if I–"

"Don't say sorry if you didn't do anything wrong." Lincoln interrupted.

Mark blinked. "...What?"

"You told me that. That day. I figured it was applicable here."

"...Oh," Mark said dumbly. "Then... it was okay?" He asked.

"I said it was," Lincoln confirmed with a nod.

Feeling relieved, but somewhat dissatisfied with that answer, Mark looked away, scratching at the back of his neck. "Then... what was that? At the staircase."

"...You picked up on my discomfort?" Lincoln asked, looking surprised.

"I... yeah. It was pretty clear." Mark said, flatly.

"Oh. I wasn't sure." Lincoln looked down. "I'm the one that should be sorry. I'm the one that brushed you off, so I'm the one that should be sorry."

"I–it's fine," Mark rushed to answer, relieved that he hadn't completely ruined their friendship. "But...why?" Lincoln wrung his hands together. "I was scared again." He said, with a sigh.

"...scared?" Mark asked, stunned. "Of me?"

"No," Lincoln replied firmly. "I was scared because I didn't know what that moment entailed for us."

"Entailed for...? Oh. *Oh*." Mark looked away, feeling himself going red.

"I... obviously, it doesn't have to mean anything, if... if you don't want to." Mark stammered. "I mean, I was– we were just–"

"Hypothetically, what if I did want it to mean anything?"

Mark snapped his head back to stare at Lincoln, his face feeling like it was on fire.

"...you... you do?" Mark asked, in a voice barely higher than a whisper.

"First of all, I said hypothetically. Second of all, I do not know. I'm sorry if that's not–"

"No, it..." Mark trailed off, screwing his eyes shut. "Honestly, I don't know either. About... any of this." He vaguely gestured between the two of them. "I mean... I think I like... but I'm not sure if I–"

"I think you were right when you said this was a bad time," Lincoln said.

That stung Mark, who looked down. "Oh. Yeah, I–"

"I think we should discuss this once we perform this exorcism," Lincoln said, holding up the bottles of holy water.

"...oh," Mark said, immediately brightening up. "I... yeah. That– that works!" He said, beginning to smile.

"Good," Lincoln said, offering Mark a smile that made his heartbeat ring through his ears.

"Okay, uh... now," Mark picked up the jug he had put down, "Let's get these to the basement."

The two walked down to the cellar, Mark feeling much lighter than he did before.

The five teenagers all sat on the floor of the cellar, as they had been for the past hour.

Axel occasionally threw curses at them. The rest of them played a couple of rounds of Go Fish with a deck of cards they found lying around. Ellie brought down a bowl of chips, and Mark had just gulped down a Dorito before Axel began to speak.

"Are you fuckers *ever* gonna let me go?" Axel snarled.

"Not for the moment, because we are not risking anything," Lincoln said, staring down at the floor from where we sat. "If you were to get possessed while we were completely unprepared, we'd be helpless."

"I don't give a fuck." Axel grumbled. "I *swear* to fuck, if you don't untie me, I..."Axel trailed off, going still. Too still.

"Axel...?" Ellie asked. "What–"

Then, something finally flashed in his eyes, and he grinned at all of them. Not sarcastically, or smugly. A genuine smile. With that, Mark realized that this wasn't Axel's grin.

"Hi, all of you." Lila looked around the room. "You know, I've been watching you guys for a while, but I've never talked to you in person." She giggled a bit to herself. "Well, in *Axel,* anyway."

"...*Lila?*" Ellie breathed.

"Yep!" She replied, with a smile.

For a moment, Mark, Lincoln, Ellie, and Rita stared at the girl in Axel's body.

"*Oh my god...*" Rita whispered, gaping at Lila. "Aunt Alita..."

"I– *holy water!*" Mark sprung up, grabbing the jug of water.

"So, you're gonna try and kill me with that, right?" Lila said, raising an eyebrow and the bottle of water. "Okay, go nuts."

"...What?" Mark stared at Lila, cocking his head.

"I mean, not *kill*, 'cause I'm already dead, but you get what I mean." Chuckling a bit, Lila leaned back against the column. "I mean, yeah, it'd *suck* if I died, 'cause I wouldn't be able to end the world, but... yeah. Well, I'll try to get out of this somehow, but..."

"Okay, *okay!*" Mark glared at Lila. "How'd you even know about the holy water?"

At that, Lila's smile faded, and she stilled, staring down at the ground.

"You know what I'm doing when I'm not possessing Axel?" When nobody responded, Lila continued. "I'm like a ghost. All I can do is walk around town, and no one– *no one*– can see me."

Lila shot a hollow grin at them. "It's been like that for the past thirty years... until Axel summoned me. *God*, it sucked." Lila chuckled to herself, an almost manic gleam in her eyes.

"But... people-watching's pretty fun, sometimes. So, I started watching you guys from the moment *you two*," Lila nodded at Lincoln and Mark. "Figured out it wasn't suicide."

Mark stared at Lila before he began to shout. "Wait– but– but why do you want to kill people? *Why'd you kill Nina and Eric?!*"

Lila shrugged. "Fish swim downstream. Just the way it is." Breathing hard, Mark tightened his grip on the bottle of holy water, twisting it open and throwing its cap somewhere forgotten on the ground.

"Wait." He felt Lincoln rest his hand on his shoulder, immediately calming him. "Lila, we have several questions, and we hope you'll answer honestly."

Lila smiled sickeningly sweetly. "Go ahead."

"Why only kill once a week? You could have killed three people at once to satisfy your goals."

Lila raised an eyebrow. "I gotta be careful. If Axel got caught– like, to the point that the mayor couldn't even cover it up– I might not get to kill the three and become an Azrog. Besides," She smiled at Mark. "It was kind of fun, watching what you guys were getting up to."

"Y–*you*...!" Mark snarled.

"Where did you get the mask the first night?" Lincoln asked, nonplussed. "

According to Mark, when you were possessing Axel and killed Eric, you were wearing a mask and a hoodie."

"Oh, that's easy." She said, giggling a bit. "That wasn't actually the first day I was possessing Axel. It was *last* week when he actually did the spell. Like I said, I didn't wanna get caught, and I had time to prepare, so..." Lila smiled to herself, her eyes glinting. "I went to the woods, and buried a knife, a rope there, and a mask."

"A knife and a rope...?" Mark's eyes widened. "That's how Eric and Nina died."

"Yep," Lila said, with a casualness that made Mark grip the bottle so hard, he felt his knuckles whiten. "Dug the stuff up, killed them, and buried all of it again."

"Okay." Lincoln nodded. "That answers all of my questions... Mark, go ahead."

Without hesitating, Mark ran up to Lila, grabbing her head as hard as he could and twisting her chin so that she was forced to keep her face up.

Managing to force her jaw open, he began to practically dump the water down her throat. He didn't hesitate for a moment, even when she was squirming violently when he heard her muffled screams.

"Mark, *Mark!*" Ellie shrieked, after what seemed like an eternity for Mark, but was really only a few minutes. "You'll *kill* Axel!"

Mark whipped around to glare at Ellie but immediately relaxed. Slowly, he turned back to Lila, and he fully comprehended the ill look on her face, excess water dripping down her chin. He looked back at the bottle. It was half empty.

"Okay," Mark said, breathing heavily. "I... I'll wait a minute. Sorry."

Ellie said something inaudible in response.

And then, the air was split by an ear-piercing scream.

"OH GOD!" Lila shrieked, her earlier cheerfulness gone and replaced with an agonized sob. "IT HURTS! IT– IT..."

A series of hellish gasps, wheezes, and rasps spilled out of her mouth. Mark couldn't find himself able to be satisfied or sickened by their sound. He didn't know which he was supposed to feel at that moment, or even if he was supposed to feel either at all.

"The holy water must be working," Lincoln said, hushed. "Let's keep going."At that, they began going in a circle, each pouring about a cup of holy water down Lila's throat, passing it down to the next person when they had done so.

"God... *please stop...*" Lila whimpered.

Ellie stared at her in horror and guilt, before opening the second jug and passing it to Rita.

As time went on, Lila's cries and movements became weaker and weaker. And then, when Lincoln had finished with his sixth cup, Lila had completely stilled.

"Lila?" Lincoln asked. "What are you–"At that, she looked up, blinking.

"What... what the hell happened?" They groaned, their voice dropping an octave. "Did– did you get rid of the demon?" They asked, perking up a bit.

"Axel...?" Ellie said, a smile sprouting across her face. "Is that really you?"

Axel glared at her. "Yeah? Why the fuck wouldn't it..." Something dawned over his face. "You got it out." Slowly, Axel began to grin. "...Holy *shit!*"

"*We did it,*" Mark said, breathless.

Mark felt a wave of relief sweep over him. Lila was gone. It was all over.

He didn't have to do any of this anymore. He could just go back to his life. He didn't have to go around, risking his life anymore– he could just be a regular seventeen-year-old, one that had a decent foster dad and a handful of friends.

Already, vignettes of what that life could be like after this began to flash through his head. He could make fun of bad movies with Ellie. Take Lincoln on a nice picnic. He even pictured Rita in the mix, sitting with the rest of the group as they laughed and chatted without aim.

"We did it," Lincoln repeated, smiling at him in a way that had Mark seriously wondering if he knew what he was thinking.

Rita laughed heartily. "Thank god... it's over." She glanced at Axel, who was still tied up. "You know what? I'm just gonna..." Walking over to Axel, she began to loosen the knot Mark had tied.

Looking at Rita, something occurred to Mark that immediately flooded out the relief he felt, dread pooling in its place.

Lincoln must've realized the same thing, as Mark could see his smile crumble out of the corner of his eye.

They both shouted for her to stop, but it was too late– the rope had already come undone, falling to the ground.

At the same time, Lila sprinted over to Lincoln's backpack, previously lying forgotten on the floor, and Mark's heart stopped when she realized what she was pulling out.

"I knew you bought your gun with you," Lila grinned, cocking it and holding it out. "I was *watching.*"

"L–Lila!?" Ellie yelped. "We... we thought you were–"

"I almost was. I gotta hand it to you, you guys almost got me!" Lila gleefully cut her off. "But, I decided to do that whole Axel bit as a Hail Mary. Turns out, I'm a pretty good actor!" Lila beamed, looking proud of herself. "I can't believe you guys fell for that! Got you guys, didn't I?"

The rest of them backed away from Lila, terrified, and Ellie began to plead. "Lila, please, whatever you're gonna do, *don't*–"

"You know what?" Lila pointed the gun at Rita. "I'm gonna start with *you.*"

"...*what?*" Rita whimpered.

"I mean, this *is* kinda your fault, that you guys lost, so... it's only fair." She grinned and narrowed her eyes.

"W–Wait! NO! DON'T–"

A loud bang sounded through the basement, and Rita's lifeless body collapsed on the ground, blood pooling from a hole in her forehead.

Everyone screamed.

Lincoln scrambled onto the ground, crouching over Rita's corpse. Ellie cupped her hands over her mouth, staring in utter horror at the scene.

Without even thinking, without even thinking about the gun, Mark sprinted over to Lila, gripping his hands around her neck. The pistol fell out of her hands.

"WHAT THE FUCK DID YOU DO, YOU PSYCHO!?" He shrieked into her face.

She let out a nauseating giggle. "I killed Rita. You know, killing's the only way to become an Azrog–"

"SHUT UP!" Mark screamed. "SHUT THE FUCK UP!"

Then, Mark shoved Lila onto the ground, kicking and punching her, desperate to alleviate the horrible, horrible feelings that had exploded inside of him.

Rita's dead. She doesn't even care. And Lila–

Mark froze, staring down at Lila in horror.

She needed to kill three people to become an Azrog. She had just done that. And now, at any moment... could she destroy the world?

Mark's blood chilled when he realized that the answer was yes.

"Oh. I..." Lila stared down at herself from the ground. "I'm slipping..."

And then, Lila blinked, and she sat up, groaning.

"What... what happened?" They groaned.

"What– WHAT DO YOU MEAN, WHAT HAPPENED!?" Mark roared.

Lila simply flinched back, looking confused in a way that couldn't have possibly been an act.

This was Axel, Mark realized.

"What the *hell*, man?" Axel growled. "*You're* the ones... that..."

Axel trailed off when he saw Rita's body splayed on the ground.

"...W–W*hat*?" He breathed. "What *the* FUCK!? Is– FUCK! SHE'S DEAD!"

"...Axel? That you?" Ellie asked weakly.

"I– what–" Axel stared down at himself, realization and horror dawning on his face. "Oh, god. It– was this *me*?"

"Lila killed her," Lincoln murmured, still staring down at her corpse.

The air went silent at that, as what had just happened fully registered with everyone.

The four gathered around her body. Mark crouched down and gingerly closed her eyes.

They watched her lifeless body for what could have been hours, none of them moving a muscle for that entire time.

"Is... is she gonna become an Azrog?" Ellie finally spoke, glancing at Axel, who sneered in response.

"There's no way of knowing for sure." Lincoln quietly replied. "Perhaps she'll never become an Azrog. Perhaps she already is one."

"Then," Axel chimed, eyes wide. "This bitch could just... kill everyone, at any time?"

"Alita." Mark finally chimed in. "We gotta drive up to Riverview, and talk to her."

"That nutcase?" Axel snorted. "Great idea."

"Oh, so you have a *better idea*?" Mark snarled.

Axel glared. "Fuck off, you bastard–"

"Mark's right." Ellie cut him off. "It might not be a great idea, but it's our one shot to figure out if we still have time to stop Lila, or... I dunno. We... we just gotta figure out what happened, and she's our best shot at that."

Axel rolled his eyes but didn't say anything.

Letting out a heavy sigh, Mark addressed the elephant in the room. "What are we gonna do about...?" He made a gesture to Rita's body.

"I..." Ellie trailed off. "I don't know."

"We should take her to Alita," Lincoln said, staring down at the body.

"I... are you sure?" Mark blinked. "Would she even want to see...?"

"I don't know if she would, no," Lincoln replied. "But she was her niece."

"But..." Ellie grimaced. "I- wouldn't that- that would just make things worse with her-"

"It might. But she was her niece. Her caretaker." Lincoln said, stubbornly.

Mark let out a long breath. "Okay. We can take her to her. But... we gotta ask her our questions first. I- if she finds out she's dead before that, we- she might not be able to answer us."

"I understand that," Lincoln replied. "Alright- all of us, let us all figure out how to get her there, and then we will ask Alita our questions."

"All-?" Axel raised his eyebrow. "What- fuck, I'm not helping." He said, sneering.

"...What?" Ellie slowly turned to him. "But-"

"Fuck this." Axel sprung up, starting towards the stairs.

"Where the *hell* are you going?" Mark growled.

"Back home. I'm not dealing with this shit."

"What- *screw you!*" Mark shouted, snarling. "This is *your* fault, you bastard!"

Slowly, Axel turned back to Mark, a hollow expression on my face.

"What did you say?" He said, his inflections making what he said sound more like a statement than a question.

"*You* summoned Lila. She wouldn't even *be here* if you didn't!" Mark threw his hands up in the air. "A-and three people died, one of them is *right fucking there*, and you have the fucking *nerve* not to help us? *What is wrong with you?!*"

Axel stared at him for an agonizing moment, a terrifyingly blank expression etched on his face.

And then, he was set off.

"My fault...?" Axel scoffed. "This- this isn't *my* fault. It's- it's LILA'S!" Axel began to rapidly close in on Mark. "You- you don't get to FUCKING-"

At that, Axel clenched his fist and swung it over his head. Mark, not regretting a word he'd said, simply screwed his eyes shut, bracing for the inevitable punch.

After a moment, it still hadn't come.

He opened his eyes just in time to see Ellie awkwardly grab Axel from behind, pulling him back a few steps at the same time that Lincoln sidestepped in front of him, spreading his arms in a protective stance.

"You may be strong, Axel." Lincoln started, looking Axel dead in the eyes. "But there are three of us and one of you. We will overpower you. As such, I do not recommend you hit Mark."

Axel stared dumbly at Lincoln, before violently shaking Ellie off of him, hard enough that she was sent staggering.

"Whatever." Axel began to start toward the stairs once again, before, abruptly, he stopped in his tracks.

"This shit wasn't my fault." Axel said. Mark scoffed in response.

"But I'm *not* gonna risk getting killed by that crazy skank." Axel walked back over to the group in an almost non-threatening manner.

"What'd you need?" Axel asked, a neutral expression on his face.

They cleaned the basement.

They washed all the blood off of Rita and the floor surrounding her. They covered up her bullet wound with a bandage they found that blended perfectly with her skin. One could be tricked into believing she was merely in a deep sleep.

"Where're you guys gonna put her?" Axel asked, with a loud yawn that made Mark want to hit him again.

"First, the bag we put you in. Then, we will put her in the trunk." Lincoln replied.

Mark shivered, knowing he'd never get rid of the image of scrubbing her blood off the floor.

Eventually, they pushed her body, now cold to the touch, into the bag, and zipped it up, before loading it into the trunk of Ellie's car. Without a word, they all got in, Ellie starting the engine.

The four-hour drive to Riverview was deafeningly silent. No one dared to say a word. Mark thought that it was for the best.

He didn't want to talk about Rita dying, Axel's presence, or anything that had happened that day. He was just tired. But he found that, even though he closed his eyes, he couldn't sleep.

When they got to Alita's building, the manager immediately ran out from behind the counter, standing in front of them.

"Hold it!" He yelled. "It's you guys again, I knew it!" He glared at Ellie. "I looked at the apartment records– there's no 'Lisa' here! You–"

Axel cut him off with a sharp glare. "Get the fuck out of our way."

The manager immediately shrank. "I- but–"

"The *fuck* did I just say?" Axel took a step toward the man, eyes flashing dangerously.

"...Go ahead." The manager immediately scampered back behind the counter.

Mark looked at him with sympathy for a moment, before following the others to the elevator. Yet again, they went back to Alita's apartment, ringing the doorbell and waiting.

After a few moments, an elderly woman showed up at the door. "Oh. Hello. I've been expecting you all."

"I... you have?"

The woman glanced off to the side. "Well, *expecting* is a strong word. But come in!"

Soon, she had them all seated on the same couch Rita had made them sit in, sitting in the same chair Rita had sat in.

"My name is Alva Fairway, and I am a long-time friend of Alita Estia. I am fully aware of her abilities, and her... condition." She tapped her fingers against the armrest of her chair. "After her niece left, and I was made to look after her, she kept saying something about a group of teenagers being our last hope." Alva's face darkened. "I'll admit, I don't know the full story, but I'm aware that whatever you are here for, it's for a good reason."

Mark looked down at the ground when she mentioned a niece. "About her niece... Rita, we... there's something we gotta tell you."

Mark, Lincoln, and Ellie all took turns, yet again relaying their tale, while Axel made obnoxious gestures.

By the time they'd finished with their story, and Mark had muttered a pitiful apology, the woman had gone completely pale.

"An Azrog... I should have known." Alva clasped her forehead in her hand, a pained look on her face. "Poor Rita... I knew her trip had something to do with all of this, I didn't think it'd go off so smoothly, but..." A single tear fell from her eye, and she let out a little whimper.

"...Alita may know things that I don't, but I believe I can help you a bit." Alva finally spoke again, wiping the tear off her cheek.

"I remember. She told me once, that an Azrog takes precisely two days to form after the ritual is completed." Alva glanced up at the four. "At around what time, did you..." She glanced distastefully at Axel, who gave her a dirty look in return.

"About ten o'clock," Lincoln said.

"Right... it's two in the morning now, so... you have about forty-four hours."

"But... how do we stop her?" Ellie asked weakly.

Alva shook her head. "If you want an answer to that, you'll have to speak with Alita."

Alva closed the door behind the four the moment they went in, staying just outside the room. Alita sat on the edge of her bed, staring at the four owlishly.

"*You*," Alita spat at Axel. "*You* bought Lila here."

Axel snarled at Alita, but Mark stepped in. "He...he didn't know what he was doing."

Alita let out a loud, uncomfortably long cackle. "No one knows what they're doing nowadays. I didn't know what I was doing when I told the People of the Nine of my visions!" She abruptly went still, her grin slipping as she stared at something unknown a thousand yards away.

"So much death... and poor, poor Lila." She turned back to Mark. "Do you know why she wants to end the world?" When Mark didn't answer, she continued. "I don't know! But, *but*, I think she considers it a mercy." Alita curled up into a ball. "She may not be aware of her motives, but it makes sense. Although, it could be one of a hundred things! Or zero!"

"Quit it, you old hag." Axel glared at her. "Tell us how to *stop her.*" She gave Axel a twisted grin. "To stop her, give her what she truly wants. Remind her. You, of all people, can do that- you're her conduit and friend."

Friend?

Mark looked over to Axel, who looked just as confused as she did.

"I- *God.*" Axel groaned. "We're not gonna get Jack out of her. Let's go." Reluctantly, Mark followed everyone else out of the room, but not before whispering a quick 'thank you' to Alita.

"She-" Mark grunted a bit, as he and Ellie carried the long black bag. "She's in here."Resting her body on the couch, the two panted a little, as Alva scrutinized the bag, before unzipping it so that Rita's head was visible.

"This'll break poor Alita's heart..." Alva said. "I'm sorry she couldn't answer your questions. But," Alva pulled out a pen and a Post-it note, scribbling a number down on it. "If you call me, I'll try to tell you as much as I know." She held the post-it out to Mark, who reluctantly accepted it. "I'd come myself, but... someone has to watch over Alita."

"What..." Ellie looked down at Rita. "What are you going to do with her?"

Mark could see Alva's face drop.

"I... I'll figure it out." She replied.

The trio expressed their gratitude and goodbyes as they left the house.

"That was a fucking bust," Axel grumbled.

"Not necessarily," Lincoln replied. "We now know that we have two days. And while Alita's instructions on how to stop Lila were vague, they were still instructions."

"Shut up." Axel snarled, before looking down at the ground. "The *fuck* did she mean when she said we were friends...?"

"Guys," Ellie yawned. "Can we talk in the car? We gotta start driving back to town..."

Rolling his eyes, Axel climbed into the car, the rest of them following suit. They discussed multiple ideas while in the car, but never came up with anything promising. They got back to Salfran Bay early in the morning and went their separate ways.

Usually, whenever Mark was stressing over something, time seemed to pass slower.

But now, with the two-day deadline loomed over him, minutes seemed to turn into seconds, hours into minutes.

The moment he started school, he was at lunch, sitting in silence with Lincoln. The moment he had finished lunch, he was back at Rick's house, sitting on the edge of his bed.

He took his sketchbook out. He had no intention of drawing anything, but he wanted to look at his old drawings to ground himself.

A flower. Some scribbles. Rick's yard.

It was ridiculous. The world could end in a day and a half, and all Mark could do was look at his stupid little pictures.

With a light scoff, he put it away again. Mark laid back on the bed, staring up at the ceiling for an hour that only felt like a second to Mark.

He only moved when he heard his phone buzz.

Lincoln: *Please come over to Ellie's house. We need to discuss and prepare our next course of action.*

Mark immediately began to type out an excuse, but when he stopped to look at what he had written, he deleted it.

Mark: *be there in 20*

Curling into a ball, Mark closed his eyes and tried to prepare himself for what was to come.

The four of them were soon gathered inside Ellie's living room.

Mark, Ellie, and Axel were on the couch, the same one where Ellie and Mark had watched that movie the other day. The two made it a point to sit as far from Axel as possible, the center of the couch unoccupied.

As for Lincoln, he paced back and forth along the living room, hands wrung behind his back as he walked around, staring down at the floor.

"Are you gonna do that forever, or do you actually have shit to say?" Axel said with a small snort. Lincoln didn't stop his pacing.

"'To stop her, give her what she truly wants. Remind her. You, of all people, can do that– you're her conduit and friend.'" He murmured to himself, repeating what Alita had told him. "What does Lila want?"

"H–hang on," Ellie chimed in, causing Lincoln to stop in his tracks. "If we have to 'give her what she truly wants...' maybe we should go over what we know about her?" Lincoln nodded.

"Okay. Thirty years ago, the People of the Nine tortured her to death..."

"And then she fucked with my head." Axel sneered.

"You're skipping thirty years," Lincoln replied.

Axel opened his mouth, undoubtedly to insult Lincoln, but Ellie cut him off.

"She said she was... basically a ghost that whole time," Ellie said, her eyes a bit wide.

Lincoln nodded. "She spent thirty years roaming around this town without anyone acknowledging her existence. Coupled with her horrific death..."

Mark stopped in his seat, as he replayed all of his interactions with Lila in his head, now taking into account the context that he had nearly forgotten.

"I... she went insane," Mark said hoarsely. "All– all that shit about fish going downstream... she lost it. And now she's..." Even with everything Lila had done, Mark felt an unmistakable sense of pity and horror creep into his chest.

"She was only fourteen..." Ellie whispered, weakly.

"The hell do we do with that?" Axel snarled.

"Let's recall what Alita said to us about Lila, again," Lincoln replied as he walked over to the rest of them, sitting on the center of the couch.

"Alita *did* say what Lila wanted– to destroy the world." Lincoln folded his hands together on his lap.

"I– we can't do that." Mark said dumbly.

"I agree with you. That is not what I meant." Lincoln stared down at the floor. "She saw it as a mercy... she figured everybody would be better off dead."The room was silent for a bit, as they mulled over what Lincoln had said.

"I– if... if I were all alone for thirty years... and I died... I– I might've–" Ellie didn't bring herself to finish her sentence.

"So that is her motive, but what does she truly want?" Lincoln asked.

"I– she wants to destroy the world, dumbass." Axel said, flatly. "The hell are you–"

"If it were that simple, Alita would have just left it at that. But she said, 'what she truly wants.'"

It was Mark that spoke this time. "She wants something else. Something Alita said that *you*," He looked at Axel from across the couch. "Could give her."

Axel immediately sprung up, his eyes flashing with rage. "I– I didn't even know what the *hell she was saying!*" He shouted venomously. "I– she said *we were friends? I never talked to her! I didn't know she was a fucking DEMON! I'm not–*"

"We know." Lincoln cut him off. "We shouldn't be taking what she was saying too literally. Perhaps what she said had some kind of hidden meaning."

Axel glared at the three of them for a long moment, before slumping back onto the couch. "The hell do you even mean by 'hidden meaning...'" he muttered.

"...Maybe she was not your friend, Axel, but maybe you were Lila's."

Axel cocked an eyebrow. "The fuck are you saying?"

"When we spoke to Lila, she mentioned watching people. Like us." Lincoln turned to Axel, making eye contact with him. "Maybe she watched you, was intrigued by you, and considered you a friend."

Axel blinked, but it was Ellie who spoke next.

"Why... why would she want *him* as a friend?"

"Fuck you too." Axel growled.

Images of what Mark had seen at the mayor's house replayed in his mind. He glanced at Lincoln, and he could tell from the look in his eyes that he was thinking the same thing as he was.

"Perhaps she saw a kindred spirit in you." Lincoln said quietly.

An unreadable expression formed on Axel's face. "What... what do you mean by that?" he asked, in a voice too flat for a question.

"Perhaps you shared a similar ordeal to her."While Lincoln didn't say what he was thinking, Axel seemed to immediately catch on to the implication. He completely froze for a long moment.

"...what the *fuck* do you know...?" Axel growled.

"Do you want me to say?" Lincoln asked in reply.

"Do- do you know about my dad?" He asked, in a dangerously low voice, and Mark's heart sped up a beat. "Fucking- ANSWER ME!" Axel suddenly roared, loud enough that Mark flinched back.

"I know that he's been abusing you, if that is what you are asking."

Axel stared at him, seething. Then, he tackled Lincoln to the ground.

"SHUT THE FUCK UP, YOU BASTARD!" Axel shrieked, wrapping his hands around Lincoln's throat.

"You- YOU DON'T KNOW JACK SHIT ABOUT ME, OR MY DAD!" Axel screamed, lowering his face down to Lincoln's.

Mark sprung up, immediately rushing to help Lincoln, but he stopped for a second, and only for a second, when he got a good look at Axel's face.

Mark had that same look on his face every time a memory of a bad home danced through his head.

Running over to the two, Mark immediately pushed Axel off of a thankfully unharmed, if rattled, Lincoln.

With a shout, Axel stood, advancing back, but the three managed to act quickly, and they ended up pinning him to the ground, while Axel thrashed and screamed awful but borderline incoherent things at them.

And then, almost as quickly as he'd been set off, he went completely still.

"...let me go." Axel said, hoarsely.

When no one responded, Axel raised his voice. "I said, *let me go*. I won't hit you or anything. I'll get out. Just let me go."

After a minute, reluctantly, one by one, they backed away from Axel, Lincoln being the last to pull away.

Sitting up, Axel stared at them. Then, he ran. In the distance, Mark heard the front door slam.

"*Jesus*..." Ellie breathed, grimacing.

"I– maybe this is good." Mark said, stuttering a bit. "We couldn't think straight with him here. This– this might be..." He trailed off at that.

In silence, the three sat back down on couch.

"So... Lila wanted to be friends with Axel cause his dad's a psycho?" Mark asked, a bit too bluntly.

"In essence, yes." Lincoln glanced at Mark. "My theory is that she thought she could relate to him, because the two of them were both suffering."

At that, they all went quiet yet again.

It was Lincoln who spoke next. "I think I know what she wants. I think I know how we can save the world." Lincoln glanced between Mark and Ellie.

"She wants a friend."

Axel didn't know how he got to Anterough City. He probably took the bus– that was how he always got there– but he wasn't sure. One moment, he was aimlessly wandering through Salfran Bay, the next, he was in this god awful city.

He lost himself in the ambience of the streets he wandered through– the smell of the car exhaust, the shrieks of traffic, the feel of the crumbled sidewalk under his shoes.

He eventually wound up sitting in an all but demolished playground, the only things still standing were a couple of benches, and a single, rusted over metal slide.

Staring around at the pathetic excuse for a park, he abruptly fell out of his dissociation. And that familiar pain came twisting into his gut.

The spell had worked. Those three figured everything out. And the world was going to end tomorrow, because of him.

And those motherfuckers all knew. About his pathetic, fucked up life.

Axel let out a shaky breath. How much did they know?

Everything?

Axel cupped his hands over his mouth. He wanted to hit something. He wanted to scream.

Axel remembered his mother. He tried desperately hard not to, but he did.

She was a beautiful woman, with almost impossibly long, golden hair, and a radiant smile. He remembered how she scooped him up in her arms, gently rocking him side to side.

He had always loved her more than the hot-tempered, perpetually frowning man that always seemed to follow them around. Who always seemed to fight with her.

He remembered one night, when he was seven, that he desperately tried to block out of his mind, but never fully could.

He'd never seen his mother cry before that day. But there she was, curled up into a fetal position on the ground, sobbing into her knees.

"Mommy...?" He stared down at her, tears beginning to form in Axel's own eyes.

At that, she looked up at him, and gave him one of her beautiful smiles. "I'm sorry, sweetie. I... I just had a bad day. That's all."

Axel's lips had parted at that. "Are you okay?" He had asked, in a comically high voice.

She shook her head. "I'm alright." She stood up, tears still streaking down her cheeks, her eyes red and puffy. "Go to sleep, baby."

Obediently, he went right to his room, turning off all his lights, ignoring how scared he was of the dark, because she hated it when he left them on, and tried to sleep.

When he woke up, he had run out to his mother's room. The door was unlocked, but when he opened it, his smile faded when he realized that it was empty.

Out of desperation, he ran to his father's room. It was locked this time. He frantically knocked on the door, and after a few minutes, it opened.

"What do you want?" The man growled.

"I–" Axel was nearly on the verge of tears. "I can't find mommy!" He cried.

At that, he froze. He'd run over to her room for a few moments, before he came running back, a phone in his hand.

He watched his father make a call, unable to make out what was happening when he could only hear one side of it. When he finally hung up, he had a scowl on his face.

"W–where's mommy?!" Axel had cried.

His father had directed his glare at him. "Kid, I don't–"It was at that moment Axel began to cry. He shrieked at the top of his lungs, crying for his mother.

And then, he felt a sharp slap against his cheek, one that sent him splayed onto the floor. He cried out as a hot flash of pain bloomed on the side of his face. He wordlessly stared up at the man, tears leaking out of his eyes.

"You want to know where she is?" He said, quietly.

The man bent down, so he was level with Axel.

"She hates us. She hates you. So, she left town."

"N—no... she can't-"

"She did." His father had begun to smirk. "She hated always having to take care of you. She hated how needy you were. And now, she's gone."

Axel screamed.

His father had never been nice, but when his mom left, he became much, much worse.

On a good day, he'd tell Axel how much of a miserable failure he was, like he already didn't know.

On a bad day, he'd throw dishes at him, or hit or kick him.

He hated it. He'd try to run away, but something or someone always bought him back, it'd just make things worse.

His parents hated him. His mom left him, and his dad hurt him.

He'd felt so worthless. He realized how pathetic and weak he was, and he hated himself for it. He couldn't run away from that.

He'd wanted to die, just to escape from it all.

But then, one day, he realized something. It was a cloudy day, about a month after his eleventh birthday.

They were at the front of city hall. He'd stood beside his father, who was giving a passionate speech about something Axel didn't understand at the time, and, even as he reflected on it now, still didn't.

He didn't care about any of that. What he remembered about that day was the crowd gathered below their platform, staring up at them. What was in their eyes varied from person to person, ranging from envy to awe to disgust to pride.

But it was clear that everybody gathered there was deeply affected by his father.

And even if he hated it, he was the son of that influential man. He had access to that power he craved.

The next day at school, he noticed an ugly, chubby girl sitting on the other side of the cafeteria.

He noted how she was already starting to form pimples, how contorted her face looked, and an urge grew inside of him, until he decided that he'd test his theory on her.

Strutting across the cafeteria, he approached her, and told her every horrible thing that he thought of when he saw her.

She cried. He laughed, and shoved her off of her seat. He was taken to the principal's office.

He'd listened to a winding, stern lecture from him, which he had all but ignored.

And then, the principal got a phone call.

Answering it right in front of Axel, he could make out his dad's voice on the other side of the phone. He couldn't hear what he said, but whatever it was, the principal had blanched, and quickly dismissed him.

He hadn't gotten into any trouble. His father had barely even cared.

And making that girl cry made him feel so great. So powerful.

It had become a pastime.

He would target anyone and everyone that looked like they could easily be picked apart. He made them suffer, and he would feel that familiar rush he adored.

But at the same time, inversely, more and more people began to turn on him. They would say horrible things about him, behind his back and right in front of him.

Just like his dad.

But unlike him, these people were easy targets. So, he simply lashed back twice as hard. Soon, almost everyone in town was terrified of saying anything to his face.

He had felt so disgustingly alive when he realized this.

Over the years, he'd graduated from making fun of a kid's gut to actively assaulting people.

If anyone so much as looked at him the wrong way, he'd beat them until his insecurities were quelled.

This was how it worked throughout the rest of middle school and all of high school.

But at the end of the day, he'd always come home to his drunk of a dad. At the end of the day, he knew he wouldn't have anything if it wasn't for that bastard.

He distracted himself from it pretty well, most of the time.

But some days, all of his negative thoughts and feelings would come boiling to the surface. Just a few weeks ago, he'd been having one of those days.

He'd come home after school that afternoon, only to face his father glaring down at him, clutching a paper in his hand.

"You got an F? In Algebra?"

"So?" Axel said, through the lump in his throat.A fist collided with his face. Axel clutched his nose in pain, gasping for air. Pulling his hand away, he could see a residue of the blood that had immediately begun to gush out of his nose smeared on his palm.

"You're eighteen." The mayor snarled. "You know who's in Algebra? Freshmen! God, you're... you're fucking pathetic!"

Scrambling, Axel shot up, sprinting over to the stairs.

He'd been through this song and dance before. His bedroom door didn't have a lock, but it had a heavy, if mostly empty, shelf conveniently right next to it. With a grunt, he pushed it in front of his door.

He lay back on his bed, grabbing a tissue from his nightstand and using it to plug up his nose, prepared to completely ignore everything his dad was about to say.

"You're a fucking ingrate, you know that?" His dad drawled, after unsuccessfully trying to kick the door down. "I give you a nice house. Food. Clothes. And you still don't give me any damn respect."

Axel rolled his eyes.

"And you're such a pansy. I mean, come on, you broke that Cooper kid's nose last month, didn't you? Do you know how much hush money I had to pay his family?" His dad said, his voice going dangerously quiet. "And you can't even take the same punch."At that, Axel snapped up, gritting his teeth.

"That's right," His father continued. "You talk a big game, Axel, I know you do, but we both know you only beat up kids smaller than you are to make yourself feel good. Cause- cause you know what, Axel? You're pathetic. And you keep getting me to clean up all of your shit, since you can't do jack on your own." He laughed hoarsely. "All you'll ever be is the son of a mayor. My son."At that point, Axel had blanched, and he felt an uncomfortable sweat drip down his palms and forehead.

His dad had left at that point, his footsteps clicking against the hard floor.

Axel stared up at the ceiling, the crushing weight of self-loathing pushing down on his chest.

From there, he spiraled, until he overturned half the things in his room, screaming obscenities to no one the whole time.

With a cackle, Axel took another swig of the whiskey he had been hiding under his bed.

He wandered aimlessly through the streets of Salfran Bay. He'd embarrassed himself, and had fun doing it. He leered and shouted at complete strangers, stumbled on the walkways in a bizarre pattern, and he laughed at himself the whole time.

Eventually, he ended up at the town library.

Axel loved this place. He loved the smell of the crisp, worn paper. He loved walking through the aisles, running his fingers down the spines of the books as he did so. He loved the absolute peace and quiet the library offered.

Stumbling inside, he heard a bell chime.

The only person in the library was a frail old woman that manned the front desk, her plaque labeling her 'Ms. Georgia.' They had spoken a few times, Axel offering her a rare amiability, or at least as close as he could get to one, but she had always looked utterly terrified of him. No guesses as to why.

"Hey, Ms. Georgia," Axel slurred. "Just... just gon' look around."

"...Okay, Axel," She rasped.

Axel turned his back, before immediately turning back to her again.

"Hey. Hey. I'm... I'm gonna ask you somethin', and I want... and I think... just, answer, and be honest. Kay?"

"Are– are you drunk, Axel?"

Axel stared at her, nonplussed, and she let out a long breath. "Alright. What do you need?"

"...Am I a good– no. Could I be a good person?" Axel asked, humming as he looked up at the ceiling. "I–"

Axel hiccuped. "I'll know if you're lying, so... so... so don't."

Ms. Georgia was quiet for a long time, before she finally answered.

"...I'm sorry, but... you've hurt this town, Axel." The woman said, with a rare firmness. "People are scared to leave their homes, because of you. I– I don't think you can... I'm sorry."Axel stared at her, feeling the expected sting of rejection.

"Right." He said, nodding. "Right. Thanks– thanks for... the, uh... honesty. Yeah." Axel laughed a bit to himself. "I'm gonna go... look, look around."

Ms. Georgia called something out after him, but by then, Axel was already too far gone, heading all the way to the back of the library.

He went into the cramped rare books section, rifling through the various shelves that were stored there.

Then, he found the manifesto, innocuously tucked next to William Salfran's autobiography.

He idly flipped through the pages, opening up to one that had instructions on how to summon an Azrog.

Then, he realized. This is what they had done to Lila.

He read more.

Today was the thirtieth anniversary of her death, wasn't it? Taking out his phone, he Googled it. It was. He could do it. Try it.

He remembered how his dad hit him. How no one in town tried to stop him. How he'd grown up without a friend, even before he got violent. What Ms. Georgia had said.

Fuck it.

Fuck this town. Fuck this world.

With a giggle, he began to read the spell aloud.

His dad was right. Everyone was right. He was irredeemable and pathetic. And he'd gotten three people killed. He was a monster.

"Hey, kid." A gruff voice from behind him spoke.

He turned around on the bench to see a woman walk up to him from his side. She was a lady that clearly hadn't aged well, with brown hair that was beginning to gray, and a body that was all saggy skin and bones.

"What." Axel said, flatly.

"Don't see kids like you out here a lot," The woman hummed, as she took an uninvited seat next to Axel. "Won't tell anyone what's going on, it's not my place." Pursing her lips, the woman turned to look at him. "But I can tell when someone's having a tough time. And if they're having a tough time, and they go to a place like this..."

"What..." Axel trailed off. "What're you getting at?"

With a sigh, the woman leaned back against the bench. "You can tell me what's happening. Go on. I won't judge."

Axel stared at her for a long moment, before softly scoffing and turning away.

"...Did you ever do something really awful?" Axel asked, softly. "And then you feel horrible about it, and you want to fix it, but you *can't*, and... you just... you..."

The woman looked at him for a long time, before staring off into space. "When I was around thirty, I drove drunk. A teenager's crippled cause of me." Slowly, Axel turned back to her. "How... how do you... live with yourself?" The woman looked up at the setting sun. "I don't really. That poor boy... I keep seeing him in my nightmares." She met Axel's eyes, her gaze softening. "If you do something shitty, you gotta live with it. For a while. Maybe even forever. But you can't block out everything else for it, either. You gotta actually do stuff. Make up for it." The woman gestured at herself. "I volunteer at soup kitchens and hospitals whenever I can. Donate blood and food, you know. And... I'm an organ donor now." The woman smiled bitterly. "I know, it's not much- and I crossed the line when I got behind the wheel that night. I know, I'm a- a piece of shit. But maybe I can at least save a life and..."

Axel let out a heavy sigh. "What- what if it's too bad? Like, you can't- you can't come back from it."

"I'm not gonna lie, there's shit you can't get back from," She conceded. "But it's better to at least try and own it than to not do jack."

Axel knew what he had to do now.

Offering a quick thanks and goodbye to the lady, he went back to the station and hopped onto the next bus to Salfran Bay.

"...Okay. Thank you." Ellie hung up the phone. "All Alva said was that Lila... she's basically dormant for now. She can't really watch or hear us till she becomes an Azrog."

Lincoln stretched. "So I suppose that means we have to convince her then. You recall the plan, correct?"

"Yeah." Mark said, scoffing a bit. "We try to make *friends* with her, cause that's apparently what she wants."

"Hey," Ellie said, a bit hollowly. "We got a shot, right?"

Mark didn't respond.

"Okay... guys." Ellie finally said. "Go home and get some rest. Check stuff off your bucket lists." She looked between the two for a long moment, before giving them a smile. "I– hey. We got this, I think. We do."

No, *we don't.*

Mark, seeing how enthusiastic Ellie looked, held his tongue and smiled at her.

The three said their goodbyes, and Mark and Lincoln started out of the villa.

The two walked side by side, moving down the street in silence.

Mark was the one who shattered the quiet. "If this doesn't work out, then- we- we're all gonna die."

"...I know." Lincoln whispered in reply.

Mark paused in his tracks, staring up at the sky, Lincoln stopping with him.

"I... it's kind of fucked," Mark said, with a hoarse laugh. "I'm not- I'm not scared. Of dying."

When Lincoln stopped to stare at him, Mark rushed to correct himself. "I mean, I am. Of course, I am. This... this is... but..." Mark shook his head. "I thought I was going to die so many times this week, it... I'm... I'm almost used to it."

"I feel the same way." Lincoln replied. Mark turned back to Lincoln, the two locking eyes, and for once, Lincoln showed no signs of looking away anytime soon. "I almost wish I was feeling more normal. And acted like I was feeling normal. I'd be writhing on the ground while I screamed. I'd be praying to God for a way out of this. Et cetera, et cetera."

Mark couldn't help but laugh a little at that.

"People always preferred normal." Lincoln said, his voice a pitch quieter. "My parents did. My classmates did."

Mark narrowed his eyes, before firmly gripping Lincoln's shoulders, pulling him a step closer. "Screw them."

Lincoln opened his mouth, but Mark talked over him.

"So–so what if you *sometimes* say or do things they don't like? I– you're still..." Sighing, Mark looked down. "You stuck by me when no one else did. You're the only reason I got through– through any of this. I... I honestly don't think I've met anyone like you." His heart pounding, he watched Lincoln's mouth fall open a bit.

"Remember what you texted me? About liking the 'real me?'" At that, Lincoln smiled a bit, and Mark grinned back at him. "Well, I like the real you, too. You're smart. You've got nerves of steel, and... and you keep saying these dumb things, and..." Mark frowned. "Wait, that, that sounded bad. You... you make me laugh. You look at things in ways I don't think I ever will, and you... it's..." Nervously, Mark chuckled a little. "I... god, you... I think you made me better. Than I was. And... I... I can't say how much that matters to me. I..."

"Mark." Lincoln said, suddenly looking at him with an intensity that caught Mark off guard.

"I... uh, what–" Mark took his hands off of Lincoln's shoulders, suddenly feeling uncertain of himself.

"Do you remember what Ellie said, just before we left?" Lincoln asked.

Mark frowned. "I– she told us that we got this, and said goodbye–"

"No, I meant just before she said that." When Mark didn't answer, Lincoln pressed. "Please answer me, Mark."

"Some– something about checking off a bucket list. Lincoln, what–?"

"Yes. A bucket list is a list of things that you want to do before you die." Lincoln cut him off. "I believe this would be applicable to mine."

Then, Lincoln wrapped his arms around Mark's back, pulling him close. Leaning up, he pressed his lips to his.

For a moment, Mark went completely still, his heart seeming to stop.

Then, it began to rapidly pound when he leaned in.

His head felt like it was spinning through the air from the feeling of Lincoln pressing against him. He legitimately forgot how to breathe for a moment, but a part of him was convinced that he didn't need to, that he could live off of just this moment for the rest of his life.

After a few minutes that passed by pitifully quickly, the two pulled away from each other, both of them, breathing hard, pressing their foreheads together.

"I think I did want it to mean anything," Lincoln finally whispered after a long moment. Mark stared at him in confusion, before he snickered, and gently smacked Lincoln on the shoulder.

"I... that's fine. I think I did too."

Lincoln smiled. "I'm glad."

Reluctantly, Mark took a small step away from Lincoln.

Lincoln's smile slowly faded. "I'm sorry, but I don't know what's supposed to happen now. Do you?"

"Come to my place."

When Lincoln looked taken aback, Mark winced. "I-not- I meant, to talk. That's it. I..." Mark looked down. "I don't wanna be alone. And after everything... I- I don't wanna just leave things like this. I'm sorry, if that's-"

"Okay." Lincoln cut him off, smiling.

Mark gazed at him for a long moment, before he smiled back at him.

The two sat in silence on Mark's bed.

Awkwardly, Mark drummed his hands on his laps, while Lincoln absently pinched and tugged at his covers.

"What is this?" Lincoln abruptly asked.

Mark looked at what Lincoln was looking at, and he gasped and grabbed it off the bed when he realized it was his sketchbook.

"I– it's just–" Mark stammered, hugging the book close to his chest. With a sigh, he cracked it open, handing it to Lincoln.

"...it's my sketchbook." Mark muttered, as Lincoln flipped through the pages. "I... I like to draw, whenever I'm feeling... off, or when I feel like it, and... yeah."Lincoln had an unreadable expression on his face when he closed the book, setting it back where he had found it.

"I know, it's stupid. I–"

"I disagree. I like your drawings." Lincoln murmured.

Mark pursed his lips. "You're just saying that–"

"You know I'm not. I'd never lie to spare someone's feelings."

"...You... you really think it's good?" Mark asked dumbly.

"Yes. A lot of heart and effort were put into the drawings." Lincoln said, firmly. "Not to mention the fact that you obviously have talent."

"I–" Mark glanced away. "Thanks."

"You are welcome."

The room went silent again. Mark stared off into space, recalling all the sketches he had drawn since he had gotten here.

And then he remembered why he had drawn them. And then, it was like he was discovering Eric's body, freaking out over Nina, and watching Rita die a cruel, unceremonious death all over again.

Why had Rita died, when Mark and all the others were in that same basement? Why did the girl that tried to help them get shot?

Why wasn't he the one to die?

It could've been him.

And it could be him tomorrow.

"Mark," Lincoln spoke up. "I don't like that look on your face. Are you–?"

"I... I think I'm having another panic attack." Mark choked out in between his quick breaths.

Lincoln immediately nodded. "Breath. Take some deep breaths. Think about the strawberries again, but this time with kiwi."

Mark shook his head. "Never... never had kiwi."

"Apples, then."Apples were sugary enough that they always left his throat the slightest bit sticky whenever he bit into one. They were always very easy or very hard to bite into, there was no in between.

"I'm here," Lincoln kept repeating.

After a few minutes, Mark's heart rate had slowed, his breathing normal again.

"Thanks... for that." Mark said, smiling at Lincoln.

"You are welcome."

After a moment of hesitation, Mark lay back on the bed. "I don't like being this vulnerable, but... I think I can trust you. No, I– I *can*."

"You can." Lincoln echoed. "And I'm happy you feel that way." He laid down next to Mark, shifting so that his side was pressed against Mark's, making his skin there buzz with warmth.

"Hey... I know this is a weird thing to ask, but... what are we?"

"You are a Mark. I am a Lincoln."

Mark laughed, staring up at the ceiling. "Come on. You know what I meant."

"Our relationship can be whatever we want it to be." Lincoln responded.

"...Do you wanna go out somewhere? If, after this is all over, and the world isn't, you know. Completely fucked."

He wasn't looking at Lincoln's face, but from the way that the surrounding air seemed to grow a little lighter, he thought he could feel him smile.

"Yes. That would be pleasant. Can I kiss you again?" Mark vigorously nodded. Lincoln rolled over so that he was facing Mark, who, for his own part, turned his head to him.

The two pressed their lips together, and for the first time since Rita's death, Mark genuinely felt happy.

For the next couple of hours, they'd kissed lazily and idly chatted about a series of completely random topics, before Rick knocked on the door and unceremoniously told Lincoln to get out.

Sliding out of the bed, Lincoln pressed a kiss on Mark's forehead, smiling at him as he left the room.

Mark went to sleep that night feeling ridiculously giddy.

With every second, Mark's stress seemed to rise exponentially.

He was practically bouncing in his seat, desperate to get out of school and actually do something to try and stop Lila from destroying everything he even remotely cared about.

But his feelings were eased somewhat when he walked into the cafeteria at lunchtime, and saw Lincoln sitting alone at their usual table. When Mark walked up to him, Lincoln caught his eye and smiled.

"Hey," Mark said, breathless.

"Hello." Lincoln said in reply.

Hesitantly, Mark sat down next to him, and held his hand out to Lincoln. He took it, and locked their fingers on the table. They simply sat there, content for a few minutes, occasionally squeezing their hands.

"I *knew it.*" A voice behind them breathed. "I *friggin' knew it!*"

They both whipped their heads around to face Ellie, grinning almost manically.

Immediately, they pulled away from each other, Mark trying and failing miserably to act casual. "Uh, hey, Ellie." Mark looked down. "What– is there something..."

At that, Ellie's face fell. "I... actually, yeah." From her pocket, Ellie pulled out a folded up sheet of paper. "This got slipped into my locker." Ellie sat down next to the two, unfolding the paper.

'*meet me behind the school @ 1:00. be there.*'

"Wait," Mark said, squinting at the note. "Do you think it's from...""Yes." Ellie and Lincoln said in unison.

"Okay... but should we– I– it's almost one."The three hesitantly looked at one another.

"It could be important." Ellie said.

Wordlessly, Mark and Lincoln glanced at each other, before nodding at Ellie.

The trio stood behind the school.

Mark crouched on the grass, while Ellie leaned against the wall. Of the three of them, Lincoln was the only one who stood upright.

"So..." Ellie grinned, gesturing between the two. "How long's this been going on~?"

"The hell are you talking about?" Mark said, rolling his eyes.

"Nineteen hours." Lincoln answered at the exact same time.

Mark glared at Lincoln.

Smirking, Ellie opened her mouth to say something, but she stopped, going pale.

Turning around, they saw Axel approaching them. He had none of the arrogance in his stride that he previously did, walking towards them in an almost casual manner.

"You came." Axel said, cocking an eyebrow.

Mark narrowed his eyes. "Yeah. But what–"

"I'm sorry." Axel murmured, not meeting their eyes.

Mark raised an eyebrow. "What–?

"*I'm sorry*," He said again, firmer this time. "It's my fault Lila killed those people. And I'm sorry that I kept picking fights with you. It was fucked up." Letting out a heavy sigh, Axel looked back up at them.

Mark and Ellie's jaws were hanging wide open. Even the usually stoic Lincoln seemed dumbfounded.

"I–" Mark finally stuttered. "Are you trying to mess with us or something? Cause if you are, I swear to–"

"No." Axel firmly cut him off, Mark saw anger flash in Axel's eyes, but it was gone as soon as it came, replaced with something that Mark couldn't name. "Look, I get that you don't like me. Fair.

I'll fuck off, if you want. But I know you probably came up with some shit in order to try and stop Lila." Axel furrowed his brows, looking momentarily conflicted, before he continued. "If you guys want, I'll help you with it."

Axel handed Mark a post-it note. Looking down at it, Mark saw it was a phone number. "If you want my help, call me. I'll go away now." Axel quickly slipped back into a school, leaving the trio utterly baffled.

Mark shook his head. "He– there's *no way* he wasn't fucking with us... right?" Mark looked between Ellie and Lincoln, both of whom stayed quiet.

Mark was jerked out of his stress induced stupor by a powerful crack of thunder.

Flinching, he looked around the classroom to see that his classmates were rushing toward the back of the room, gathering around the window.

Quickly, Mark got up and ran over, writhing through the crowd of students until he could see what everyone was staring out at.

He gasped a little when he saw the sheer amount of rain that was pouring down from the sky, lightning flashing out of nowhere every few moments. Looking down to the ground, he could see trees on the verge of uprooting from the winds that he could hear screeching even from inside the school.

Just a few minutes ago, it'd been a slightly chilly, but sunny day.

"This is easily the biggest storm to hit Lewis county for decades," the newscaster said, clearly rattled. "We urge you, if you live in Lewis, Catherine, or River county, seek indoor shelter. We repeat, seek–" At that, the audio slowed, to the point of becoming inaudible, and the TV screen filled with static.

"*Fuck*," Rick glared at the TV, shaking his head. "Antenna must've got knocked out."

Mark grunted in response, heading to his room and opening his messages.

Lincoln: *Have you all seen the storm outside?*

Ellie: *dude, how could we NOT see it*

Mark: *do you guys think this has anything to do with lila?*

Lincoln: *It likely does.*

Lincoln: *It's seven o'clock. She is supposed to reach her full power at eight.*

Lincoln: *Perhaps this is a sign of the process starting.*

Mark: *this is just it starting?*

Mark: *god, we're fucked.*

Lincoln: *Not if the plan works.*

Ellie: *Stupid question– how do we even go about getting Lila's attention?*

Ellie: *do we just run around town and hope for the best*

Lincoln: *I suppose so.*

Lincoln: *I can't think of any other options.*

Mark had begun to type out a reluctant agreement, knowing full well how high the risk of them failing was.

...you want... meet?

Mark froze, hearing a high-pitched, but raspy voice echo through his head.

Though, 'hearing' might not have been the right word for it. Mark was immediately reminded of all the times that he'd been falling asleep, and he'd begun to partially fall into a dream while still conscious. Then, he was somehow able to hear something from that dream while simultaneously being able to recognize that it was entirely in his head.

...don't know why... but come... Greenwater fields.

"...Lila...?" He quietly uttered.

Yes...

"Wait– hello? Can, can you?" Mark frantically looked around the room, but got no response.

"Fuck..." Mark opened his phone again, quickly typing out a message to Lincoln and Ellie.

Mark: *no. we gotta go to greenwater fields*

Ellie: *what? Why?*

Mark: *i heard lila's voice.*

Mark: *in my head*

Mark: *i think she was trying to communicate with me*

Mark: *she said to go there to talk to her*

Ellie: *...she can mess with people's heads?*

Lincoln: *Yes. It makes sense because in an hour, she'll be powerful enough to destroy the world.*

Ellie: *okay. we gotta get there. Now*

Ellie: *i'll pick you guys up. be there in a few*

Mark and Lincoln both typed out an okay.

Rifling through his stuff and putting on his warmest coat, Mark began to start out his room, before something occurred to him.

Hesitantly, he clicked his phone on once more, inputting the number Axel gave him.

Mark: *if you were serious about what you said, get down to greenwater as soon as possible*

Turning his phone off, Mark headed out.

"Where the *hell* are you going?"

Mark stopped in his tracks, the hand reaching out to open the door freezing midair.

He turned around, nervously hiding his hands behind his back. "I– I was just–"

"Kid, the winds are more than sixty miles an hour out there! You can't just go out!"

"I–" Mark glanced at the door, before shaking his head. "Ellie's driving, she's picking me up–"

"I *don't care!*" Rick cut him off. "The weather's already bad, and it's only going to get worse from here. We're probably gonna have to evacuate tonight!"

"Rick. This is– you– I have to go out." Mark stammered.

Something in Rick's face shifted at that.

"It's more than just the moving, or the dead bodies." Rick murmured. "It's– what's happening, Mark?"

"I–" Mark stared down at the ground. "I can't tell you. You wouldn't even believe me if I did."

"...Try me."

Mark stared up at Rick, and it was clear from the look on his face that he had meant what he said, and was prepared to listen to what he had to say.

Mark opened his mouth, but before he could say anything, he heard the honk of a car horn from outside.

Jerking his head around, he looked out the window and recognized Ellie's car.

At that moment, Mark knew what he had to do.

"If I make it back, I–I'll explain everything," Mark said, turning back to Rick. "Thank you, for… for everything. Taking me in. Therapy. Talking. I… you're a good guy."

At that, Mark sprinted out the door and slammed it behind him, ignoring Rick's yelling.

Lincoln stared out the window, waiting for the telltale silver BMW to park outside. The car that would drive him out to the field where he and his friends would either save the world, or die trying.

"Linky?" His mother called out for him.

"What is it?" He replied, not looking away from the window.

"I'm making mac and cheese! It'll be ready in an hour."

"Alright. Thank you for letting me know."

Marleene whistled a bit, before walking over to Lincoln and looking out the window.

"It's a scary storm, isn't it?"

"Yes. Do you believe that I can go to Harvard?"

Marleene blinked, laughing a little. "What?"

"Let me rephrase my question. Do you believe that I can go to Harvard, and succeed there?"

"Of- of course I do! If you try hard enough, you can do anyth-"

"That's a pleasant sentiment, but it's just not true. Some goals are unattainable for me, even if I try my best to obtain them. For example, I'll never be able to ride a magic unicorn, or go skateboarding on a rainbow. Is attending Harvard, with relatively few issues, one of those goals?"

"Don't- don't be silly, Linky. Of course, you can go to Harvard!"

"What makes you think that?"

"...what?"

"Why, specifically, do you think that I can go to Harvard?"

"I-well, you study hard. You're at the top of the class- like you said, you'll probably make valedictorian! And you've been doing really well on those SAT practices, I'm really proud of you for that..."

"Do you know what I want to major in?"

"Huh?"

"Do you know what I want to major in, when I get to university? If so, tell me what I want to major in."

"It's– it's engineering, right?"

"That's incorrect. I want to major in law."

"I'm sorry, Lincoln, I didn't–"

"I forgive you. But I'd like to point out that I've pointed out my interest in attending law school many times. I mentioned it over dinner three days ago."

"I– Lincoln, I didn't– I wasn't sure if you were being serious?"

"Did you think that because you don't believe I *can* be serious?

"What– what do you mean?"

Lincoln could faintly make out Marleene's increasingly distressed look in her reflection in the window, and a part of him relished in it.

"Mom. How much of what I say do you take seriously?"

"...I– sweetie, look at me."

Lincoln turned around to face his mother, but he didn't meet her eyes.

"Of course I take you seriously! Always."

"I know you're lying."

"No I'm not! I– you're my son, Lincoln. I always listen to you."

"We've had similar conversations to this, and I ended all of them at around this point, either because I believed that you would permanently change your behavior, or because I simply didn't have the will and energy to continue the conversation. But this time, I know that you won't change unless I keep talking, and I do have the will and energy to do so. Mom. I don't think that you take me seriously, in general, but specifically, I don't think you recognize what I've achieved scholastically. I have the best grades and test scores in my class, by a landslide. I've won multiple, mostly fairly prestigious, scholarships and academic competitions. Every single one of my teachers adore me– as a student. Maybe not as a person. It's impressive for me to have accomplished all of that. But it always feels like you don't realize how impressive it is. You always act proud, but you act proud in the same way that you acted proud when I was eight and I got my flu shot, and I didn't cry before or during. Except that I'm not eight, and I haven't been for nine years."

The room went silent for a bit as Lincoln tried to figure out how to articulate what he wanted to say next. Marleene opened her mouth, but Lincoln cut her off before she could say anything.

"I think I know why you don't act so proud." Lincoln said quietly. "When I was 10, and I got my diagnosis, I noticed your behavior changing. You began to treat me like there was something seriously wrong with me. To be fair, there *is* something wrong with me, and it's probably serious. No, I misspoke. I might be exaggerating, but you began to treat me almost like I was a lost cause. Like there wasn't hope for my future. So you think that *anything* that demonstrates the fact that I can function as something adjacent to a normal person is equal cause for celebration. Be that a 1600 on the SAT, or me holding my own in a somewhat intelligent conversation. But in the end, you still, perhaps unconsciously, look down on me for being aut–"

"*Lincoln!*" His mom wailed, and Lincoln finally looked up to meet her eyes, and he saw tears welling up in them. He felt guilty for making her cry, while somehow simultaneously not regretting a word he had said.

"That's not true! O–of course it isn't! I'd– I'd never look down on you for something like that! Or at all! I–" Marleene trailed off, staring at Lincoln.

"You really believe all of that, don't you?" She asked, her voice barely above a whisper.

"I do."

"Lincoln- I- I'm sorry." Marleene said, her voice shaky. "But you're my *son*. Of course I'd-" She squeezed her eyes shut.

"When that bully, when she hurt you- it- I was so worried about you. The doctors were telling me that you might die. After the surgery, all they could talk about was how lucky you were that you didn't have any lasting brain damage."

"I know all of this."

"...Yeah. I guess you do." Humorlessly, Marleene laughed a little. "But- Lincoln- I never stopped worrying. I just- I never want you to get hurt like that ever again, so I just- when you got your diagnosis, I just wanted to protect you-"

"I think I understand, mom." Lincoln cut her off. "And for what it's worth, I appreciate the intent. But I wish that you didn't have to treat me like a child in order to feel like I'll always be safe."

"That's not... Lincoln... I don't know. I *don't*."

"What don't you know?"

"How to protect you! How to be a good mom, how to make you happy- any of it!" Marleene put her face in her hands, and, hesitantly, Lincoln put a hand on her shoulder.

"I should have been more tactful when expressing myself. I'm sorry."

"No, Lincoln- I- *I'm* the one that needs to be sorr-"

"Maybe you should be sorry, but so do I. While I've tried talking to you about my feelings about all of this before, I should've expressed all of what I just said a long time ago." Lincoln paused.

"...I should've tried to relate to you more. I'm bad at that."Marleene smiled sadly at Lincoln. "I think you got that from me."

"It's possible." Lincoln said, smiling back.

"...We have to talk more. About how we feel, about what we really think."

"I agree."

Marleene opened her mouth to say something else, but then, a car honked outside.

She stared out the window in disbelief. "Why on earth is anyone driving in this weather?"

"I'm sorry. I have to go." Lincoln sprinted to the front door, grabbing his jacket off the coat rack. "Later, we can talk more about what we were just talking about, and I'll explain what I'm doing right now. But now, I have to go. I love you, mom."

Before Marleene could react, Lincoln sprinted out the door and into Ellie's car.

"Step on it!" Lincoln shouted, as he watched his mother start out the house. Ellie obediently drove off. Lincoln pulled his phone out from under his coat, and texted Marleene.

Lincoln: *I'm sorry for making you worry. I promise you, I'm safe, and I'll explain everything later. Again, I love you.*

Lincoln put his phone back into his jacket, and stared at Ellie for a while.

"Hello."

"...Hi." Another long silence ensued, before Ellie spoke up again.

"...so we're really doing this?"

"Yes. Are we going to pick up Mark now?"

"Y–yeah. It should take about 5 minutes."

Lincoln stared out at the raging storm as he thought about Mark.

He thought about how he made more of an effort to understand and sympathize with Lincoln than almost anyone else he ever knew, and succeeded, even though Lincoln knew he never made it easy for him. He thought about how, even after everything he'd been through in life, he was willing to make himself vulnerable for Lincoln. He thought about how much Lincoln knew he cared, no matter how hard he tried to hide it.

Then, Ellie stopped the car, and he saw Mark running through the rain. To *him*.

He remembered kissing him outside Ellie's house, curling up next to him on his bed.

If the world is going to end, at least Mark will be by my side for it.

At that thought, Lincoln let himself smile a little.

Mark pushed his way through the sheets of rain pouring down and the gusts of wind that almost knocked him over, and practically dived into Ellie's car, immediately slamming the door shut, breathing hard.

"You made it." Lincoln was sitting in the back of the car, right next to him.

Mark offered him a small smile as they drove off.

"It's a ten-minute drive from here." Ellie said, glancing up at the rearview mirror. Mark could see the fear and uncertainty in her eyes.

All things considered, the car ride was uneventful, but the audible whistling of the wind, along with the sight of several collapsed signs and trees, made the anxiety pooling in Mark's chest spike.

At one point, a trash can was knocked over, rolling into the street. Ellie was forced to swerve to avoid it. Mark had flinched, his heart racing.

Seemingly sensing Mark's momentary panic, Lincoln wordlessly took Mark's hand in his, rubbing circles into it with his thumb. The gesture quickly calmed him down, and he squeezed Lincoln's hand in return. Their hands stayed intertwined for the rest of the drive.

After a few more minutes, they began to drive along a dirt road, and they parked the car where it ended, in the center of the field– which was a massive, but essentially empty, plain of grass that stretched out into the distant horizon.

They stayed put in the car, the weather not having improved, and Ellie glanced at her phone.

"It's 7:15 right now." She commented.

Mark pursed his lips, looking out the windows, around the field.

"Mark, are you looking for something in particular?" Lincoln asked, tilting his head a bit.

"I– yeah. I actually told–"

As if on cue, he heard a horn honk from behind them.

Looking out the rear window, he saw a car coming to a stop behind them.

Axel rushed out of it, tapping on the window next to Mark. Scooting over, he unlocked the door and let him slip in.

"Axel?" Ellie gawked. "What're you doing!?"

"I told him to come." Mark answered in Axel's place. "Texted him."

"I– *Mark.*" Warily, Ellie glanced at Axel. "This could be dangerous. He–"

"What– what do we have to lose?" Mark cut Ellie off. "We need all the help we can get."

Axel stayed quiet, looking out the window.

"...Fine. You're right." Pursing her lips, Ellie glanced around the car, trying to look out of all the windows. "But... what–?"

...Get out... car.

Mark froze, feeling his blood chill. Glancing around at everyone else's faces, it was clear he wasn't the only one to have heard the voice.

"That... that was Lila." Ellie said.

Mark nodded. "I... should we–?"

"I suppose."

Mark looked outside. The storm seemed to have gotten worse since he had gotten into Ellie's car. Hesitantly, he cracked the door open to be met with a roar of wind. Climbing outside, with the sheer amount of rain pouring down, he might as well have been jumping into the ocean.

The wind had slowed down a bit, at least. But even with the heavy coat he had donned, it was freezing. Clenching his jaw, Mark tried to stop his teeth from chattering, to little avail.

"*Fuck*, it's cold..." Axel groaned.

Ellie rubbed her arms, visibly shivering.

And Lincoln was covering his ears, seemingly unfazed by the weather.

"The wind is too loud," he explained to Mark.

Mark stared at Lincoln in disbelief, but didn't question him.

*...Hear me? Can you hear me better?*Mark blinked. It was the most coherent Lila had been since she'd started talking in his head.

"Yes, we can." Lincoln said, reluctantly lowering his hands from his ears.

"Good."

Mark froze. It was unquestionably Lila's voice, but it didn't have the same dreamlike quality it had before– it was live, ringing through his ears rather than his head.

Whipping his head, he saw her.

She was undeniably the girl he'd seen when he'd typed her name into Google– she had the same round face, the same gap in between her teeth. Hell, she even wore the same kind of 'good girl' outfit she did in the pictures– a snugly fitting plaid shirt, with a knee-length black skirt and matching suspenders.

"Um... hi!" Lila greeted them, a sheepish smile on her face.

"*...Lila?*" Ellie gawked at the girl that had been standing right behind the four. "*How–?*"

"My powers as an Azrog got a lot stronger!" Lila looked down at herself, as if her body personally fascinated her. "It's almost like I'm back in my body..."

"I– Lila–" Mark choked out. "You– even if you can– don't– don't *do this*."

Lila shook her head. "Sorry, I gotta! I–"

"Why?" Lincoln cut her off. "Why do you want to destroy the world?" She rolled her eyes, as if Lincoln had just asked the stupidest question she had ever heard.

"I *told you*, It's just how it is–"

"Except, that's not what we think is really happening." Lincoln fiddled with the bottom of his coat, as he stared directly at her.

Lila's smile faded. "What–" She blinked, as she stopped for a second. "What're you talking about?"

"We think that this, all of this," Lincoln made a vague gesture at the rain falling down from the sky, "Is your own way of coping with the misery and trauma that you've been facing for the past thirty years.

Lila stared at Lincoln, her eyes wide.

Then she laughed.

"Oh, *please!*" Lila said, between cackles. "I'm not some *baby*. Me dying, the haunting... it's all in the past, you know–"

"Except it isn't." Lincoln interrupted her. "Because even if what happened to you is over, you are still suffering from what happened to you."

At that, Lila froze, before glaring at Lincoln.

"Come on. You don't know what you're talking about."

"Yes, I do."

She glowered at Lincoln for a few more minutes.

Then, she smirked, and twisted her hand in the air.

And then, Lincoln fell on his knees, nails digging into the ground as he began to scream in agony.

"*Lincoln!*" Mark immediately rushed over to him, crouching down beside him. Lincoln simply continued to wail.

Mark turned to snarl at Lila. "What the *hell* did you do to him?" He spat.

Lila giggled, before making another twisting motion with her hand.

At that, Lincoln stopped screaming, and was left panting, as he relaxed himself, before, woozily, he stood up again.

"What *was that?!*" Mark shouted at Lincoln.

"Please don't yell at me," Lincoln said, pain still etched on his face. "I don't know. But everything hurt."

"Maybe that'll teach you to stop saying stuff like that. Not knowing what your talking about."

Mark stared at Lila, a sense of horror creeping over him.

If she could do that to Lincoln so easily, there was nothing stopping her from killing them all at any time. Nothing but their words.

"So," Lila said, crossing her arms over her chest. "You guys wanted to convince me *not* to destroy the world." Lila rolled her eyes. "I... I kind of want to hear what you guys wanna say! I'm not changing my mind, but knock yourselves out, anyway!"

"...Lila," A rough voice spoke.

It was Axel, staring at Lila with a pained look.

"Don't... you don't wanna do this." Axel said, hoarsely.

Lila pouted. "But *you're* the one that summoned me, Ax!"

"I- that was-"

"C'mon, you *know*— you get where I'm coming from." The mocking tone in Lila's voice was replaced by a quiet genuineness. "I- we're the same, aren't we? We- we were both being- and we don't *want* this- any of this-" Lila spread her arms out wide. "To keep going. You- you of all people get that, don't you?"

"...No." Axel bit out. "No. This isn't what you want, and- and you know it. You were hurt, and- you wanted to feel better. So... so you did all of this. But this- this won't make you happy. You- you'll just be hurting people. It won't. I- trust me. I- I've *been there*."

Lila was silent for a long moment, the wind and rain the only sounds filling the air.

"It's not *about* me being happy." She finally said, in a voice scarcely above a whisper. "I- people out there- *they're in pain!*" She glared, beginning to shout. "They're *suffering!* I- *I can't just leave them!*" A hysterical grin formed on her face. "No one tried to save me from those *bastards*. No- no one tried to save me when I spent *thirty years* wandering around town. Hell, everyone forgot about me! And- and if anyone else is just- *like that*- I- I- I HAVE TO SAVE THEM!"

With a roar, she sliced her hand through the air, and suddenly, they were surrounded by a ring of fire, unfettered by the current storm, that towered over all of them, crackling threateningly.

In terror, the four living packed closer together.

"Why- why do you all look *scared*?" Lila shouted, enraged. "Dying- dying *for real*- it's a good thing, *isn't it!?* You don't have to *hurt, or feel, and-*" Lila cut off with a gasp, and for a long moment, she stared at something a hundred miles behind Mark.

"I- wanted it all to end. When they were hurting me, when I was spending all of those years in the town... I was so desperate." Lila looked back at them, and Mark saw the utter despair in her eyes, and he didn't see a demon, or a murderer, or a maniac- he saw the tortured and scared child that she was.

"Why... why do people like living, or feeling, so much?" Lila asked, hoarsely. "I might've... once... but I can't really remember."

"...I like living and feeling because I have things and people that I love, and people that love me in return." Lincoln replied. "If you liked life, that's probably why. When you had those people and things taken away from you, and they were replaced with nothing but pain, that's also probably why you hate it now."

"I- things and people I love..." Lila smiled, looking utterly broken. "It- everything hurt too much. I can't remember them."

The living watched Lila in silence, who was completely lost in thought.

"I think I loved my friends." Lila finally said. "I don't remember them. But I played games with them, and I loved them." Lila stared off into space, the fire still crackling around them. "I lost them all after... all I could do was watch them forget about me, even though I was *there*..."

"...I want a friend." Lila finally spoke again. "That would make me happy, I think."At that, the flames surrounding them died. The rain stopped too, but the wind was still blowing strong.

"I– Lila..." Ellie stared at her in pity. "We..."

"We can be your friends." Lincoln said. He pulled out a deck of playing cards from his pocket, the packaging visibly damp, but otherwise unharmed. "Would you like to play a game? I think that is what friends do."

Lila stared at the cards, before looking around at the others. "You'd... you'd do that?" Ellie, Axel, and Mark looked among themselves, and nodded.

Wordlessly, Lila sat on the ground, patting next to herself. The living four circled up with her.

"Can we play Mao?" She whispered.

Axel cocked his head. "The fuck is that?" He asked, as the rest agreed.

Pursing his lips, Axel turned to Lila. "...Okay. How do you play?"

Ellie grinned mischievously at the rest of the living. "So, funny thing about Mao…"

"Failure to say have a nice day," Lila said, grinning at Axel.

"JUST TELL ME THE GODDAMN RULES!" Axel roared, throwing his cards down on the ground. Everyone else, despite themselves, laughed.

"I'm sorry, but it is tradition to have to figure it out on your own." Lincoln replied in a serious voice, though Mark could see that his lip was twitching.

Laughing, Mark glanced at Lila. They locked eyes for a long moment, before they awkwardly looked away from each other at the same time.

Even if it began as a ploy to stop Lila, after several hours of card games, banter and teasing, Mark could honestly say he was having fun. He didn't know what to make of that.

He knew how much Lila had suffered. He knew that she was borderline insane from everything. But he also knew that Eric, Nina, and Rita had died at her hands.

Before he could ponder for too long, Ellie let out a whoop. "I win!"

"Failure to say Mao," Lincoln said, putting a card in front of her.

"Fuck!" She said, in an equally cheerful voice. Everyone- even the still moody Axel- laughed again.

"Mao." Lincoln said after a couple of moments, holding his empty hands up.

"Okay, good game," Mark said, chuckling a bit. He watched Lila stare off into space, a tiny smile on her lips.

"I... you all wanted to be my friends, even after everything..." Lila started.

"Lila...?" Ellie asked, hesitantly.

"This is why I liked life so much." Lila said, a smile starting to form on her face. "Having people that talked to me... cared about me... that's..." She looked down. "That's what I really wanted, for all that time."

Then, her face clouded over with melancholy. "I... I was trying to take... take *this*," Lila gestured at the now abandoned cards, "Away from people." She shook her head. "I'm... I'm horrible. Even if there are people suffering... there are just as many people that love their lives. Love other people. And I tried to take it all away." She hung her head, tears beginning to stream from her eyes. "I... I'm no better than *those people*... I-"

"Lila." Mark said. "You- you're *nothing* like those people. You... you've been... and-" Mark met Lila's eyes. "What you did was wrong. But... but you... you wanted to help people, didn't you?"

Slowly, Lila nodded at Mark.

"Then... that makes you better than a lot of people," Mark said, finally.

Lila stared at Mark, before a smile crept up on her face. "Th- thank you... Mark... *all of you.*" Lila looked around at the others.

"Today was... was one of the best days, for me." Lila looked down at herself. "You guys are my friends... and-" Lila cut herself off.

"I can't go through with the plan." Lila whispered.

"You- you won't?" Ellie said, smiling.

"I- I can't. People, they- they *need* to live. I needed you guys to see that." Then, Lila smiled sadly down at herself. "But I don't."

Mark's smile faded. "Lila, what-"

"I- thirty years." Lila looked down. "It's... it's too much time. I... don't think I can ever really be... *happy* after that."

"What- yes, you can!" Mark protested, shaking his head at Lila. "Lila, you- you can start a new life, somewhere. You-"

"I- it's been too long." Silently, tears began to stream from her eyes yet again. "I could live in a *mansion,* with a ton of friends and family, and- and *everything* I ever wanted, but–" Lila let out a heavy sigh. "I– I spent so long, wanting for it to all end, I– I don't think I can ever want anything else."

"Lila," Mark said, dread creeping up on him. "What– what're you saying?"Lila looked down, before standing up.

"Hey, what–?" Mark sprung up, along with everyone else.

"I– I don't know what'll happen if I do this, so... take a few steps back, okay?"

Lincoln was the only one to obey this request. Mark, Axel and Ellie stayed put, staring at Lila.

Then, something invisible gently pushed them back to where Lincoln was standing.

"Lila, what– *what're you doing!?*" Mark yelled, struggling against the force.

Lila walked away from them, until she was about twenty feet from the group.

"Thank you all!" Lila called.

And then, Mark was blinded by an impossibly bright light, and a deafening screech rang through his ears.

Just like that, it was all over.

Mark blinked his eyes open. The weather was back to normal– the sun was setting, and the air felt gentle on his skin, if a bit chilly.

But he barely even noticed any of that, because when he looked ahead, he saw that Lila was gone.

"Wh- Lila!" Mark sprinted towards where Lila was standing. "She's- where'd she go?"As Mark kept shouting, the others walked over to him.

"Do you not get it?" Lincoln asked, interrupting him mid-yell. "She destroyed herself."Mark froze, and simply turned to stare down at the spot where Lila had stood when she had thanked them.

"She didn't have the will to exist anymore." Lincoln muttered, quietly.

"She- she's gone..." Mark said numbly.

Lila wasn't a part of this world anymore, in any shape or form. She never got to experience a normal life past her fourteenth year.

It was all over. But Mark didn't feel a shred of the relief he had thought he'd feel.

He was just tired. Looking around, he could tell the others were just as exhausted as he was.

"...I want to go home." Lincoln muttered. Ellie and Mark nodded in agreement. The three started back toward the cars, but Axel stayed put.

"...Axel?" Mark called, just as he was about to open the car door.

"I... I don't wanna go back." Axel said. "I *don't*."

Ellie tilted her head. "I... go back to Salfran Bay, or...?"

"Any of it. Salfran Bay, my dad's house, I..." Axel walked over to the rest of them.

"I've got about a thousand bucks in the trunk, and the gas tank's full." Axel said, nodding at his car. "I'm leaving town. I– I'll figure out what to do next.

"Wait, you can't just..." Mark trailed off, and stared at the completely despondent look on Axel's face.

"...Okay. Go." Mark said with a sigh.

Axel nodded at him, before walking over to his car. Standing in front of its door, he turned back to them.

"For what it's worth... I really am sorry. For everything." He murmured, before opening the door.

"*Wait.*" Lincoln called, just as Axel was about to climb inside the car.

"We have proof of the fact that the mayor was abusing you." Lincoln said. "We can share it with the town. He'll go to jail."

Slowly, Axel turned back to them, before giving Lincoln a curt nod.

Then, he got into the car and drove off.

After a few moments, the rest of them got into Ellie's car.

During the drive back, something snapped inside of Mark, and quietly, he began to cry. Without saying anything, Lincoln wrapped his arm around Mark, and they stayed like that until they were back in town.

"...That's basically everything that happened." Mark finished.

Rick rubbed his temples. "I- kid, what the *hell?*"

"Call Ellie. Or Lincoln. They'll tell you the exact same story."

"This isn't funny, Mark-"

"It's not supposed to be."

"You- no. No. You can't just expect me to believe all that crap. I'm sorry, Mark, but you-"

"Don't give me that." Mark said in a low voice. "You wanted to know what happened, I told you what happened."

"No *you didn't!* You just told me a fucking movie. That's not-"

"How else do you explain all the shit that happened over the past few weeks?! The, the 'suicides', the huge fucking storm that came out of *nowhere*, and Lila-"

"*Don't!*" Rick angrily cut him off. Mark glared up at him, a scathing retort on the tip of his tongue, but it died when he saw that, Rick looked more distraught than anything else.

"I... I don't know, I-" Rick suddenly stood from the table. "We... I need to think. We can talk more later."

Rick walked off, and Mark faintly heard the front door open and close.

After spending the evening drawing in his sketchbook, Rick came back just as Mark was about to slip into bed.

"I'm sorry." He said, his voice hoarse. "I should've listened, you've been through a lot– I just– I couldn't believe everything. And I– god. I wish I'd done *something* while you were doing all this."

The two of them talked for the rest of the night, Mark recalling more details about everything that happened at Rick's prompting. When Mark finally decided to go to bed, Rick promised that he believed everything that Mark told him. Mark had no idea if he was telling the truth or not.

Then, he said he'd do better for him in the future.

Maybe Mark was naive for it, but he completely believed that part.

As Mark walked down the halls of the school, he heard hushed whispers all around him, though, for once, the commotion didn't seem to revolve around him.

His heart skipped a beat when he caught the word *'mayor.'*

He eventually found Ellie by her locker, who gave him a small, exhausted smile.

"Do... Do you know what's going on?"

"Apparently, *someone* uploaded some... incriminating recordings from the mayor's house onto all the town's social media."

"I'm that someone." From out of nowhere, Lincoln popped up from behind her. "As was implied. It turns out, him abusing his child didn't even scratch the surface of his depravity."

"What... happened after that?"

"He has been detained by the Lewis County Police Department. He is being questioned as we speak."

Mark went quiet. Somehow, even after everything, he felt no catharsis. How could he, when the mayor could be suffering fates a hundred times worse than this one?

He closed his eyes, taking a long, deep breath, feeling the storm in his mind calming down a little.

Then, he looked at his best friends, and smiled.

"Hey, Ellie. Hey, Lincoln."

"Hey." Ellie replied breathlessly.

"You did this out of order. Also, hey."

Mark laughed a little, before looking down at his feet.

"It's really over, huh? Everything. All the supernatural shit, it..."

"Yeah..." Ellie sighed.

"So we just... move on? Forget this ever happened?"

Lincoln pursed his lips. "Unless I get dementia when I'm older, I doubt I'll ever forget this."

Mark snorted. "Right..."

"Also, I don't want to forget this."

Ellie looked a little taken aback at that, but she nodded. "I- I don't think I want to, either."

"I- neither do I." Mark shook his head. "This was all... this fucked me up, don't get me wrong... but... I- I guess, *something* came out of it- I don't know."

"I think I feel the same way, Mark." Lincoln replied. "We should remember this- for our own sakes, and Eric's, and Nina's, and Rita's, and Lila's."

Mark nodded. Ellie opened her mouth to say something, but then the bell rang, and the three went to class.

School was finally over, and Mark wanted nothing more than to go home and collapse in his bed. He stood in front of the school, waiting for Rick to come and pick him up, when a voice startled him.

"Hello, Mark."

Mark jumped. "Fuck, Lincoln."

"Sorry." Lincoln said, looking away from him. "Anyway, will you go on a date with me tonight?"

Mark blinked. "What?"

"You asked if I wanted to go out with you when everything was over. I said yes. If it's a bad time, I understand, but will you?"

Lincoln was as expressionless as always, but Mark saw the red in the tips of his ears.

"Y–yeah. Sounds good."

"Good. I'll text you the details later." Lincoln awkwardly stared at Mark for a little bit, like he was waiting for him to do something, before he leaned in and gave him a quick kiss. Lincoln nodded to himself, before walking away.

Mark unconsciously bought a hand up to his lips, scoffing as an idiotic grin spread across his face.

Mark lied back in his bed, as his phone rang beside him. Just as he was convinced it would go to voicemail, Ellie finally picked up.

"Hey, Mark!"

"Hi, Ellie. I just wanted to call, see how you were dealing with... everything."

"Uh... well, all things considered, pretty well. I think I'll be alright." Ellie paused for a bit. "I still might need therapy, though."

Mark laughed a little. "Same here. Not about the therapy stuff. I mean, yes, that too, but- yeah. I think I'll be okay."

"G-good. Good to hear."

The line went silent for a while, before Ellie spoke again.

"Hey, Mark?"

"Yeah?"

"We're... we're still gonna be friends, right?"

"What?" Mark shot up. "What are you talking about? Of course we're still friends! Why-"

"I know, I know- I just." Ellie sighed a little. "I mean, if it weren't for Lila and Axel... honestly, we probably wouldn't have become friends."Mark opened his mouth to argue, but realizing the truth in her words, he closed it.

"And we were mainly spending time together in order to try and figure out how to... save the world- *fuck*, this was all insane. I- sorry. Yeah, there were those times we hung out together, but... I- I dunno-"

"Ellie. Stop." Mark lied back down, staring at his phone. "I-I get it. But you're wrong. I still want to be friends. I still wanna watch Pink Princess with you, talk shit about the girls at our school, I– all of that."

"...You mean that?"

"Yeah."

"We're gonna stay friends?"

"Yeah."

"Actual friends. Like, we don't just say hi to each other in the halls for a month, then never talk to each other again."

"Actual friends, yeah." Mark felt a smile creeping up on his face.

"I'm gonna hold you to that."

"Go ahead."

Mark heard Ellie take a deep breath before she spoke again.

"Good. Good. Now... I saw you and Lincoln talking earlier."

"A–and?" Mark tried to sound nonchalant, but his stammer failed him.

"Saw you kiss." Mark could hear Ellie's shit-eating grin in her voice.

"So?" Mark rubbed his hands over his face, which had turned beet red. "He asked me out, okay?"

Mark winced as Ellie squealed at a frequency that nearly made his ears bleed.

"Aw... mister dark-and-brooding's finally learning how to love again!"

"Fuck you."

Ellie laughed, before her tone turned sincere.

"Seriously, though. I'm happy for you, man. Both of you."

"...Thanks."

"So... where are you two going?"

"He said he'd tell me, but I–"

As if on cue, his phone buzzed.

"...That him?"

"Yeah." Mark opened his texts.

Lincoln: *Meet me at the top of Silvercrest hill at 6:00 PM.*

Mark: *k. see you.*

"Looks like we're going to Silvercrest hill."

Ellie laughed. "God, didn't know Lincoln was such a romantic."

"Huh?"

"Silvercrest hill is *gorgeous* at sunset."

"...Oh." Once again, Mark felt his face warm. "Gotta go. I– I'll talk to you later."

For the first time in an embarrassingly long time, Mark took a shower. He scrubbed every inch of his skin raw, making sure that he smelled like a garden.

He put on the nicest clothes he owned– a black polo and blue jeans– and left the room. He ran into Rick in the living room.

"You're looking sharp." Rick said, his brow raised.

"Y–yeah, well…" Mark scratched at the back of his neck, not meeting Rick's eyes. "I got a date."

"Oh. I– huh." Rick looked thoughtful. "Didn't think you really had that kind of stuff on your mind."

"I… I guess it is kinda weird." Mark said, laughing a bit.

"Is it with that girl? Ellie? I guess it makes sense, you did spend all that time together."

Mark tensed.

"Uh… no."

"Then who? You only really hung out around Ellie and–" Rick's eyes went wide. Mark hated every second of the silence that ensued.

"Shit."

"Yeah."

"With *him*?"

"…Yeah."

"…okay then. Have fun."

Mark blinked. "What?"

"Go. Go on your date. Have fun."

Mark immediately felt himself relax, and he smiled at Rick, his trust in him once again renewed.

"Thanks."

Mark started out the living room, and Rick called out to him.

"You can stay out till 12 tonight."

Mark turned back to see Rick smiling at him fondly.

"You earned it."

Mark ran the entire way up the hill, not caring for the fact that his legs already ached from walking there in the first place.

"I'm sorry I'm late. I had to-" Mark froze, his throat going dry as he took in the sight before him.

Lincoln was sitting criss cross on a striped blanket spread out on the ground below him, a weaved basket at his side. He wore a pair of khaki shorts and a white dress shirt, a black bow tie around his neck. His hair had a bit of gel in it, so his curly hair looked slightly more ruly than usual.

"Hey."

"Hello." Lincoln looked Mark up and down. "Sit with me."

Mark quickly sat on the blanket, facing Lincoln, drawing his knees to his chest.

"A... a picnic?" Mark asked dumbly.

"Yes, this is a picnic." Lincoln put the basket between the two of them, taking the lid off of it.

Inside was a large Tupperware container filled with pasta, a bowl of watermelon and cantaloupe, and a large glass bottle of sparkling water.

"If it was legal, I would've gotten champagne." Lincoln pulled out two wine glasses and poured into them, handing one to Mark.

"Wow. This– this is…" Mark felt his heart race. "You did all this for me?" He asked, his voice a note higher than it usually was.

"No. I also did it for myself. I like picnics." Lincoln paused for a bit, before his eyes widened, like he remembered something. "But I also did it for you. Mainly for you. Primarily for you. I–"

"I– I get it, man." Mark smiled at Lincoln, who tentatively looked him in the eye and smiled back. "This is… really, really great. I… thank you. For doing this."

"You're welcome."

Mark held up his glass. "Cheers?"

Lincoln nodded. "Cheers."

They clinked glasses, and drank. Setting his glass down, for a long moment, Mark simply watched Lincoln, who was still sipping his water.

The setting sun shined down on him in the best way possible, making his skin glow, and his slightly slicked hair glisten. It highlighted the shadows under his eyes, and the calm, focused look in them.

Lincoln glanced up at him, and Mark quickly looked away, but there was no way he didn't see that he was staring.

"Either I have something on my face, or you think I look good. I hope and think it's the latter."

Mark flushed, but still grinned like an idiot. "It's the latter."

"Good." Lincoln pulled the pasta out of the basket. "After we're done eating, let's make out."

It was official. Mark was in love.

Lincoln was curled up against Mark's side, his head resting on his chest, one arm slung over his stomach. The sun had fully sunk into the horizon, and with that came the cool night air, so the warmth of his body was all the more welcome.

Mark was on the verge of falling asleep when Lincoln spoke up.

"Mark?"

"Yeah?"

"Do you want to talk about the past few weeks?"

Mark stilled for a bit, before sitting up at the same time Lincoln did. He moved away from him a little, but the two of them were still side by side.

"What- what about them?"

"How you feel about what happened. How they affected you."

"I-" Mark shook his head. "How do you *think* they affected me?"

"Negatively, overall. But if you're comfortable, I'd like to hear specifics."

"I- I don't-" Mark pursed his lips. "I- guess I know where you're coming from, I do, but- I didn't really think I'd have to talk about all that tonight. Or- or *think* about it. I just- I don't know."

"If you want, I can apologize, we can pretend like I didn't ask you anything, and we can go back to cuddling."

Mark couldn't help but laugh at that, though the air remained tense as a silence hung between the two of them.

"I just... I feel angry. Eric, Nina, Rita, *Lila*... none of them deserved the shit that happened to them. They... they all had lives ahead of them, a-and it just pisses me off. And I can't even blame anyone for what happened. Hell, I can't even blame fucking *Axel*, not after everything! Just- it was all so awful, and it happened for no good reason and I can't–" Mark broke off, feeling tears well up in his eyes.

Lincoln wordlessly rested his head on Mark's shoulder, as he tried desperately hard to stop crying. But every time Mark was convinced he'd calmed down enough to try talking again, he remembered some god awful detail about the past few weeks, and he broke down again. Eventually, he gave up trying to stop.

When Mark finally ran out of tears to cry, Lincoln's head was still on his shoulder.

"Do you feel better?" Lincoln said, as he bought a hand and rubbed Mark's back.

"A little." Mark replied hoarsely, his voice a little raw from his sobbing. "I–I'm sor–"

"If you're going to apologize for crying, I won't let you do so."

In spite of himself, Mark giggled. "Alright."

The two leaned against each other for a while, not speaking, before Lincoln broke the silence." I think you should speak to your therapist about all of this."

"Yeah, I– wait, no. Then they'd–"

"Sorry, I misspoke. Not all of this. I'm saying that you should change the details of your story so that it's more believable, and share that version with your therapist."

"Change...? How would that even–"

"For example, You could say Lila was an old acquaintance of yours who you recently learned died in a car accident. You could change the constant threat of death that followed you for the past month into general anxiety involving school. Et cetera."

"What?" Mark shook his head. "I get what you're saying, but there's no way that'll work– I– I think."

"You might not get the exact treatment you need, but is it not worth a shot?"

"I–" Mark pursed his lips. "Okay. I'll try it."

"Thank you for that." Lincoln pulled away from Mark so he could smile up at him. Hesitantly, Mark reached out to cup his cheek in his hand. The two stared into each other's eyes for a long moment.

"You know, save for that last bit, I had a great time tonight." Mark said, his voice barely above a whisper.

"So did I. Let's do it again, soon."

"Does... does that mean we're dating now?" Mark felt like a preteen girl asking that, but any and all embarrassment was pushed into the back of his mind in favor of his giddiness.

Lincoln's normally pale skin flushed as he replied.

"Yes."

Mark leaned in to kiss him again.

One year later

Mark was standing just outside the school when he felt a pair of arms hug him tightly from behind.

"Hey," Mark said, turning to face Lincoln, who looked absolutely giddy. "Someone's in a good mood." He noted with a chuckle.

"As I should be." Lincoln grinned, puffing out his chest a little. "I just spoke to Ms. Muff– she said that I'm all but a shoo-in for Harvard University."

Mark's eyes widened. "Really? Shit, that's great!" Grinning, Mark grabbed Lincoln again and kissed him.

"Hey," He whispered, leaning into Lincoln's ear. "Proud of you."

"Thank you." Mark could hear how happy he was in just those two words.

"Hey!" A voice shouted from behind them. "Ix-nay on the D-A-Pay!"

The two immediately sprung apart, both of them turning to scowl at Ellie.

"That is not how pig Latin works." Lincoln grumbled.

"Aw, come on." Ellie laughed. "You know I'm just teasing!"

Mark rolled his eyes.

"So, uh..." Ellie looked down. "It's been a year since, uh..."

"Y-yeah." Mark said, the air immediately sobering.

"Let's go." Lincoln said, glancing between the two of them.

They had designated the day that Lila had destroyed herself as an anniversary of everything that had happened that month.

They had written out a plan a month ago, and that day, they followed it.

First, they headed to Riverview, and paid their respects to Rita, and, once again, thanked Alita and Alva for all their help. They were all pleased to find that, according to Alva and their own observation, Alita was getting a bit better.

Then, late at night, they headed back to Salfran Bay, where they left flowers at Lila's grave. Her tombstone was dirty and worn, to the point that they could barely read the name on it, but it was there.

After laying out the bouquet of roses, they stayed at Lila's grave for a long time, before, eventually, the groundskeeper had told them to leave.

The first part of the walk back to the car was silent, but Lincoln abruptly spoke up.

"What do you think happened to Axel?" Lincoln asked.

"I... I dunno." Ellie said. "I– I *hope* he got everything together. Maybe he found a job, got a place..."

"I hope so too." Lincoln murmured. "But it's just as likely he's living in misery right now. Or he killed himself. Or he reverted back into his old habits."

Despite everything that he had done, at the end of the day, they all felt sympathy for Axel, in the same way they did for Lila. Mark sometimes found himself desperately wishing that it was Ellie's prediction that was right, and not Lincoln's. But he couldn't deny the possibility that it wasn't.

"...You're right." He conceded.

In another long stretch of silence, they climbed back into Ellie's car.

"I don't want to go home and sleep, just yet." Lincoln blurted. "Ellie, can we go to your house?"Mark and Ellie shared the sentiment. Ellie's parents were conveniently gone again, so they drove over to her villa.

The three of them watched more of Ellie's kiddie cartoons. They found themselves laughing at the screen while they made snarky comments to one another, and the mood between the three was lightened.

"...Hey." Mark said, when Ellie had finally turned the TV off. "I love you guys."

Ellie and Lincoln turned to stare at him.

"...I wasn't expecting that." Lincoln said finally.

"I know, after today, this is kinda bad timing, but..." Mark scratched at the back of his neck. "And I know, I haven't said things like this before, but... I do. You- you guys were my rock, this past year, and... I never had people *like* you guys in my life. I-"

"I love you too, Mark." Lincoln cut him off, smiling at him.

Mark gaped at him for an embarrassing moment, before he smiled back.

"I love you too!" Ellie chimed in. "Not in the gross way Lincoln does, but I still do!"Mark laughed while Lincoln deadpanned. "That is homophobic."

"You *know* I just hate romance in general." Ellie pouted, before her face softened. "Seriously, though. I love you, man."

Mark felt almost unbearably warm. He grinned at the two. "I– thanks, guys."

After a long, comfortable silence, Ellie spoke up. "You guys wanna watch the new Pink Princess movie again?"

"Yes." Mark grinned, springing up.

"I'm surprised the franchise hasn't been killed." Lincoln muttered.

Ellie smiled, before grabbing the remote and clicking it on.

Ellie had forced them to watch this movie a thousand times before, so none of them were particularly invested in the plot. They simply sat side by side on the couch, facing the screen, comfortably enjoying the calm, but pleasant moment.

Eventually, Mark looked around him to find that Lincoln and Ellie were both fast asleep. Chuckling to himself, he clicked off the TV.

He pressed a kiss onto Lincoln's forehead, before leaning back against the couch, closing his eyes.

I think I'm okay, Mark thought, as he drifted off to sleep.

Acknowledgements

I can't stress enough what a wonderful journey writing and publishing this book was, and howmuch I appreciate the people that helped this project come to fruition.

First, I would like to thank my mentor, Shan. In all those Saturdays when we met up at Panera, you've always given me wonderful advice that shaped my work ethic and gave me confidence in the ability I had to achieve my goals.

Second, I'd like to thank my amazing mother and father for always keeping me in line and ensuring that I got all my work done. Without them, I'm sure I would have procrastinated into oblivion.

Third, I need to thank my proofreaders– dad again, my sister Sara and my classmate, Edina. I'd like to give special thanks to Edina, who took the effort to write hundreds of notes that helped me totally transform the book for the better.

Finally, I would like to thank my beautiful shih tzu and de facto little brother, Dumpling, for always being there for me to snuggle whenever I was struggling.

About the Author

Naomi Stebbins is an up-and-coming author who is very happy to be able to release her debut novel. She hopes she can one day reach people through her stories and change their lives. In addition to writing, she enjoys music, art, and cuddling with her pet Shih Tzu, Dumpling.